Henry James

Henry James OM (15 April 1843 – 28 February 1916) was an American-British author regarded as a key transitional figure between literary realism and literary modernism, and is considered by many to be among the greatest novelists in the English language. He was the son of Henry James Sr. and the brother of renowned philosopher and psychologist William James and diarist Alice James.

He is best known for a number of novels dealing with the social and marital interplay between émigré Americans, English people, and continental Europeans. Examples of such novels include The Portrait of a Lady, The Ambassadors, and The Wings of the Dove. His later works were increasingly experimental. In describing the internal states of mind and social dynamics of his characters, James often made use of a style in which ambiguous or contradictory motives and impressions were overlaid or juxtaposed in the discussion of a character's psyche. (Source: Wikipedia)

Literary works:

Watch and Ward (1871)
Roderick Hudson (1875)
The American (1877)
The Europeans (1878)
Confidence (1879)
Washington Square (1880)
The Portrait of a Lady (1881)
The Bostonians (1886)
The Princess Casamassima (1886)
The Reverberator (1888)
The Tragic Muse (1890)
The Other House (1896)
The Spoils of Poynton (1897)
What Maisie Knew (1897)
The Awkward Age (1899)
The Sacred Fount (1901)

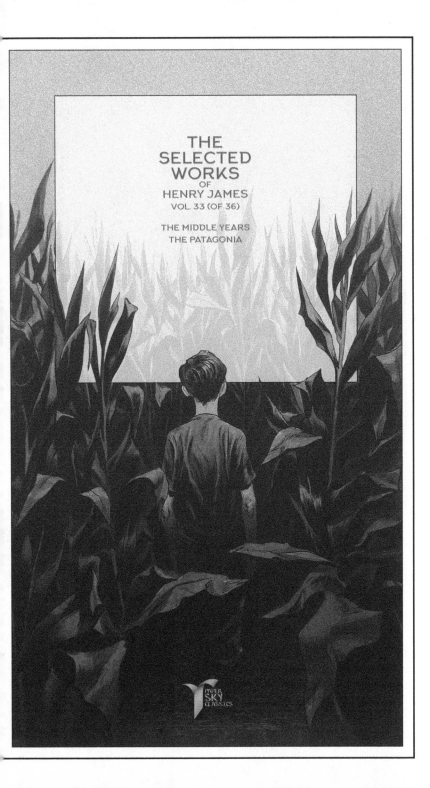

THE SELECTED WORKS

OF

HENRY JAMES

VOL. 33 (OF 36)

THE MIDDLE YEARS
THE PATAGONIA

PAPER SKY CLASSICS

An Imprint of Papersky Classics LLC

A Wholly Owned Subsidiary of Queenior LLC

A Melodragon Company

First Printing: 2020

ISBN 978-1-6627-1768-0 (Paperback)

ISBN 978-1-6627-1769-7 (Hardcover)

Published by Papersky Classics

www.paperskyclassics.com

Contents

THE
SELECTED
WORKS
OF
HENRY JAMES
VOL. 33 (OF 36)

THE MIDDLE YEARS

EDITOR'S NOTE

The following pages represent all that Henry James lived to write of a volume of autobiographical reminiscences to which he had given the name of one of his own short stories, The Middle Years. *It was designed to follow on* Notes of a Son and Brother *and to extend to about the same length. The chapters here printed were dictated during the autumn of 1914. They were laid aside for other work toward the end of the year and were not revised by the author. A few quite evident slips have been corrected and the marking of the paragraphs—which he usually deferred till the final revision—has been completed.*

In dictating The Middle Years *he used no notes, and beyond an allusion or two in the unfinished volume itself there is no indication of the course which the book would have taken or the precise period it was intended to cover.*

PERCY LUBBOCK.

!

If the author of this meandering record has noted elsewhere[1] that an vent occurring early in 1870 was to mark the end of his youth, he is moved here t once to qualify in one or two respects that emphasis. Everything depends in uch a view on what one means by one's youth—so shifting a consciousness is his, and so related at the same time to many different matters. We are never ld, that is we never cease easily to be young, for *all* life at the same time: outh is an army, the whole battalion of our faculties and our freshnesses, our assions and our illusions, on a considerably reluctant march into the enemy's ountry, the country of the general lost freshness; and I think it throws out t least as many stragglers behind as skirmishers ahead—stragglers who often atch up but belatedly with the main body, and even in many a case never atch up at all. Or under another figure it is a book in several volumes, and ven at this a mere instalment of the large library of life, with a volume here nd there closing, as something in the clap of its covers may assure us, while nother remains either completely agape or kept open by a fond finger thrust n between the leaves. A volume, and a most substantial, *had* felt its pages ery gravely pressed together before the winter's end that I have spoken f, but a restriction may still bear, and blessedly enough, as I gather from nemory, on my sense of the whole year then terminated—a year seen by me ow in the light of agitations, explorations, initiations (I scarce know how ndearingly enough to name them!) which I should call fairly infantine in heir indifference to proportions and aims, had they not still more left with ne effects and possessions that even yet lend themselves to estimation.

[1] "Notes of a Son and Brother," 1914.

It was at any rate impossible to have been younger, in spite of whatever nevitable submissions to the rather violent push forward at certain particular points and on lines corresponding with them, than I found myself, from the first day of March 1869, in the face of an opportunity that affected me there and there as the happiest, the most interesting, the most alluring and beguiling that could ever have opened before a somewhat disabled young man who was about to complete his twenty-sixth year. Treasures of susceptibility, treasures not only unconscious of the remotest approach to exhaustion, but, given the dazzling possibilities, positively and ideally intact, I now recognise—I in fact long ago recognised—on the part of that intensely "reacting" small organism; which couldn't have been in higher spirits or made more inward fuss about the matter if it had come into a property measured not by mere impressions and visions, occasions for play of perception and imagination, mind and soul, but by dollars and "shares," lands and houses or flocks and herds. It is to the account of that immense fantastication that I set down a state of mind so out of proportion to anything it could point to round about save by the vaguest of foolish-looking gestures; and it would perhaps in truth be hard to say whether in the mixture of spirit and sense so determined the fact of innocence or that of intelligence most prevailed. I like to recover this really prodigious flush—as my reader, clearly, must perceive I do; I like fairly to hang about a particular small hour of that momentous March day—which I have glanced at too, I believe, on some other and less separated page than this—for the sake of the extraordinary gage of experience that it seemed on the spot to offer, and that I had but to take straight up: my life, on so complacently near a view as I now treat myself to, having veritably consisted but in the prolongation of that act. I took up the gage, and as I look back the fullest as well as simplest account of the interval till now strikes me as being that I have never, in common honour, let it drop again. And the small hour was just that of my having landed at Liverpool in the gusty, cloudy, overwhelmingly English morning and pursued, with immediate intensities of appreciation, as I may call the muffled accompaniment for fear of almost indecently overnaming it, a course which had seated me at a late breakfast in the coffee-room of the old Adelphi Hotel ("Radley's," as I had to deplore its lately having ceased to be dubbed,) and handed me over without a scruple to my fate. This doom of inordinate exposure to appearances, aspects, images, every protrusive item almost, in the great beheld sum of things, I regard in other words as having settled upon me once for all while I observed for instance that in England the plate of buttered muffin and its cover were sacredly set upon the slop-bowl after hot water had been ingenuously poured into the same, and had seen that circumstance in a perfect cloud of accompaniments. I must have had with my tea and my muffin a boiled egg or two and a dab of marmalade, but it was from a far other store of condiments I most liberally helped myself. I was lucidly aware of so gorging—esoterically, as it were, while I drew out the gustatory process; and I must have said in that lost reference to this scene of my dedication which I mentioned above that I was again and again in the aftertime to win back the homeliest notes of the impression, the damp and darksome light washed in from the steep, black, bricky street, the crackle of the strong draught of the British "sea-coal" fire, much more confident of its function, I thought, than the fires I had left, the rustle of the thick, stiff, loudly unfolded and refolded "Times," the incomparable truth to type of the waiter, truth to history, to literature, to poetry, to Dickens, to Thackeray, positively to Smollett, and to Hogarth, to every connection that could help me to appropriate him and his setting, an arrangement of things hanging together with a romantic rightness that had the force of a revelation.

To what end appropriation became thus eager and romance thus easy one could have asked one's self only if the idea of connectibility as stretching away and away hadn't of a sudden taken on such a wealth of suggestion; it represented at once a chain stretching off to heaven knew where, but far into one's future at least, one's possibilities of life, and every link and pulse of which it was going accordingly to be indispensable, besides being delightful and wonderful, to recognise. Recognition, I dare say, was what remained, through the adventure of the months to come, the liveliest principle at work; both as bearing on the already known, on things unforgotten and of a sense intensely cultivated and cherished from my younger time, and on the imagined, the unimagined and the unimaginable, a quantity that divided itself somehow into the double muster of its elements, an endless vista or waiting array, down the middle of which I should inconceivably pass—inconceivably save for being sure of some thrilled arrest, some exchange of assurance and response, at every step. Obviously half the charm, as I can but thinly describe it, of the substantially continuous experience the first passages of which I thus note was in the fact that, immensely moved by it as I was, and having so to deal with it—in the anticipatory way or to the whatevers and wherevers and whenevers within me that should find it in order—I yet felt it in no degree as strange or obscure, baffling or unrecognising on its own side; everything was so far from impenetrable that my most general notion was the very ecstasy of understanding and that really wherever I looked, and still more wherever I pressed, I sank in and in up to my nose. This in particular was of the perfect felicity, that while the fact of difference all round me was immense the embarrassment of it was nil—as if the getting into relation with the least waste had been prepared from so far back that a sort of divine economy now fairly ruled. It was doubtless a part of the total fatuity, and perhaps its sublimest mark, that I knew what everything meant, not simply then but for weeks and months after, and was to know less only with increase of knowledge. That must indeed have been of the essence of the general effect and the particular felicity—only not grotesque because, for want of occasion, not immediately exhibited: a consciousness not other than that of a person abruptly introduced into a preoccupied and animated circle and yet so miraculously aware of the matters conversed about as to need no word of explanation before joining in. To say of such a person that he hadn't lost time would, I knew, be feebly to express his advantage; my likeness to him, at any rate, probably fell short of an absurd one through the chapter of accidents, mostly of the happiest in their way too, which, restraining the personal impulse for me, kept appearances and pretensions down. The feast, as it more and more opened out, was all of the objective, as we have learned so comfortably to say; or at least of its convenient opposite only in so far as this undertook to interpret it for myself alone.

To return at all across the years to the gates of the paradise of the first larger initiations is to be ever so tempted to pass them, to push in again and breathe the air of this, that and the other plot of rising ground particularly associated, for memory and gratitude, with the quickening process. The trouble is that with these sacred spots, to later appreciation, the garden of youth is apt inordinately to bristle, and that one's account of them has to shake them together fairly hard, making a coherent thing of them, to profit by the contribution of each. In speaking of my earliest renewal of the vision of

Europe, if I may give so grand a name to a scarce more than merely enlarged and uplifted gape, I have, I confess, truly to jerk myself over the ground, to wrench myself with violence from memories and images, stages and phases and branching arms, that catch and hold me as I pass them by. Such a matter as my recovery of contact with London for a few weeks, the contact broken off some nine years before, lays so many plausible traps for me that discretion half warns me to stand off the ground and walk round it altogether. I stop my ears to the advice, however, under the pleading reminder that just those days began a business for me that was to go ever so much further than I then dreamed and planted a seed that was, by my own measure, singularly to sprout and flourish—the harvest of which, I almost permit myself to believe, has even yet not all been gathered. I foresee moreover how little I shall be able to resist, throughout these Notes, the force of persuasion expressed in the individual *vivid* image of the past wherever encountered, these images having always such terms of their own, such subtle secrets and insidious arts for keeping us in relation with them, for bribing us by the beauty, the authority, the wonder of their saved intensity. They have saved it, they seem to say to us, from such a welter of death and darkness and ruin that this alone makes a value and a light and a dignity for them, something indeed of an argument that our story, since we attempt to tell one, has lapses and gaps without them. Not to be denied also, over and above this, is the downright pleasure of the illusion yet again created, the *apparent* transfer from the past to the present of the particular combination of things that did at its hour ever so directly operate and that isn't after all then drained of virtue, wholly wasted and lost, for sensation, for participation in the act of life, in the attesting sights, sounds, smells, the illusion, as I say, of the recording senses.

What began, during the springtime of my actual reference, in a couple of dusky ground-floor rooms at number 7 Half-Moon Street, was simply an establishment all in a few days of a personal relation with London that was not of course measurable at the moment—I saw in my bedazzled state of comparative freedom too many other relations ahead, a fairly intoxicated vision of choice and range—but that none the less set going a more intimately inner consciousness, a wheel within the wheels, and led to my departing, the actual, the general incident closed, in possession of a return-ticket "good," as we say, for a longer interval than I could then dream about, and that the first really earnest fumble of after years brought surprisingly to light. I think it must have been the very proportions themselves of the invitation and the interest that kept down, under the immense impression, everything in the nature of calculation and presumption; dark, huge and prodigious the other party to our relation, London's and mine, as I called it, loomed and spread—much too mighty a Goliath for the present in any conceivable ambition even of a fast-growing David. My earlier apprehension, fed at the season as from a thousand outstretched silver spoons—for these all shone to me with that effect of the handsomest hospitality—piled up the monster to such a height that I could somehow only fear him as much as I admired and that his proportions in fact reached away quite beyond my expectation. He was always the great figure of London, and I was for no small time, as the years followed, to be kept at my awe-struck distance for taking him on that sort of trust: I had crept about his ankles, I had glanced adventurously up at his knees, and wasn't the moral for the most part the mere question of whether I should ever be big enough to so much as guess where he stopped?

Odd enough was it, I make out, that I was to feel no wonder of that kind or degree play in the coming time over such other social aspects, such superficially more colourable scenes as I paid, in repetition as frequent as possible, my respects and my compliments to: they might meet me with wreathed smiles and splendid promises and deep divinations of my own desire, a thousand graces and gages, in fine, that I couldn't pretend to have picked up within the circle, however experimentally widened, of which Half-Moon Street was the centre, and nothing therefore could have exceeded the splendour of these successive and multiplied assurances. What it none the less infinitely beguiles me to recognise to-day is that such exhibitions, for all their greater direct radiance, and still more for all their general implication of a store of meaning and mystery and beauty that they alone, from example to example, from prodigy to prodigy, had to open out, left me comparatively little crushed by the impression of their concerning me further than my own action perhaps could make good. It was as if I had seen that all there was for me of these great things I should sooner or later take; the amount would be immense, yet, as who should say, all on the same plane and the

ame connection, the æsthetic, the "artistic," the romantic in the looser sense,
r in other words in the air of the passions of the intelligence. What other
assions of a deeper strain, whether personal or racial, and thereby more
uperstitiously importunate, I must have felt involved in the question of an
ffective experience of English life I was doubtless then altogether unprepared
o say; it probably came, however, I seem actually to make out, very much to
his particular perception, exactly, that any penetration of the London scene
vould *be* experience after a fashion that an exercise of one's "mere intellectual
uriosity" wherever else wouldn't begin to represent, glittering as the rewards
o such curiosity amid alien peoples of genius might thoroughly appear. On
he other hand it was of course going to be nothing less than a superlative
elp that one would have but to reach out straight and in the full measure of
ne's passion for these rewards, to find one's self carried all the way by one's
ctive, one's contemplative concern with them—this delightful affair, fraught
vith increase of light, of joy and wonder, of possibilities of adventure for the
nind, in fine, inevitably exhausting the relation.

II

Let me not here withal appear to pretend to say how far I then foresaw
myself likely to proceed, as it were, with the inimitable France and the
incomparable Italy; my real point is altogether in the simple fact that they
hovered before me, even in their scrappy foretastes, to a great effect of ease
and inspiration, whereas I shouldn't at all have resented the charge of fairly
hiding behind the lowly door of Mr. Lazarus Fox—so unmistakeably did it
open into complications tremendous. This excellent man, my Half-Moon
Street landlord—I surrender, I can't keep away from him—figures to me now
as but one of the thousand forms of pressure in the collective assault, but he
couldn't have been more carefully chosen for his office had he consciously
undertaken to express to me in a concentrated manner most of the things
I was "after." The case was rather indeed perhaps that he himself by his
own mere perfection put me up to much of what I should most confidently
look for, and that the right lines of observation and enjoyment, of local
and social contact, as I may call it, were most of all those that started out
from him and came back to him. It was as if nothing I saw could have done
without him, as if nothing he was could have done without everything else.
The very quarters I occupied under his protection happened, for that matter,
to swarm—as I estimated swarming—with intensities of suggestion—aware
as I now encourage myself to become that the first note of the numberless
reverberations I was to pick up in the aftertime had definitely been struck
for me as under the wave of his conducting little wand. He flourished it
modestly enough, ancient worthy of an immemorial order that he was—
old pensioned servant, of course, of a Cumberland (as I believe) family, a
kind, slim, celibate, informing and informed member of which occupied
his second floor apartments; a friend indeed whom I had met on the very
first occasion of my sallying forth from Morley's Hotel in Trafalgar Square
to dine at a house of sustaining, of inspiring hospitality in the Kensington
quarter. Succumbing thus to my tangle of memories, from which I discern no
escape, I recognise further that if the endlessly befriending Charles Nortons

introduced me to Albert Rutson, and Albert Rutson introduced me to his feudal retainer, so it was in no small degree through the confidence borrowed from the latter's interest in the decent appearance I should make, an interest of a consistency not to have been prefigured by any at all like instance in my past, that I so far maintained my dizzy balance as to be able to ascend to the second floor under the thrill of sundry invitations to breakfast. I dare say it is the invitations to breakfast that hold me at this moment by their spell—so do they breathe to me across the age the note of a London world that we have left far behind; in consequence of which I the more yearningly steal back to it, as on sneaking tiptoe, and shut myself up there without interference. It is embalmed in disconnections, in differences, that I cultivate a free fancy for pronouncing advantageous to it: sunk already was the shaft by which I should descend into the years, and my inspiration is in touching as many as possible of the points of the other tradition, retracing as many as possible of the features of the old face, eventually to be blurred again even before my own eyes, and with the materials for a portrait thereby accessible but to those who were present up to the time of the change.

I don't pretend to date this change which still allows me to catch my younger observation and submission at play on the far side of it; I make it fall into the right perspective, however, I think, when I place it where I began to shudder before a confidence, not to say an impudence, of diminution in the aspects by which the British capital differed so from those of all the foreign together as to present throughout the straight contradiction to them. That straight contradiction, testifying invaluably at every turn, had been from far back the thing, romantically speaking, to clutch and keep the clue and the logic of; thanks to it the whole picture, every element, objects and figures, background and actors, nature and art, hung consummately together, appealing in their own light and under their own law—interesting ever in every case by instituting comparisons, sticking on the contrary to their true instinct and suggesting only contrast. They were the *opposite*, the assured, the absolute, the unashamed, in respect to whatever might be of a generally similar intention elsewhere: this was their dignity, their beauty and their strength—to look back on which is to wonder if one didn't quite consciously tremble, before the exhibition, for any menaced or mitigated symptom in it.

I honestly think one did, even in the first flushes of recognition, more or less so tremble; I remember at least that in spite of such disconcertments, such dismays, as certain of the most thoroughly Victorian *choses vues* originally treated me to, something yet deeper and finer than observation admonished me to like them just as they were, or at least not too fatuously to dislike—since it somehow glimmered upon me that if they had lacked their oddity, their monstrosity, as it even might be, their unabashed insular conformity, other things that belong to them, as they belong to these, might have loomed less large and massed less thick, which effect was wholly to be deprecated. To catch that secret, I make out the more I think of it, was to have perhaps the smokiest, but none the less the steadiest, light to walk by; the "clue," as I have called it, was to be one's appreciation of an England that should turn its back directly enough, and without fear of doing it too much, on examples and ideas not strictly homebred—since she did her own sort of thing with such authority and was even then to be noted as sometimes trying other people's with a *kind* of disaster not recorded, at the worst, among themselves.

I must of course disavow pretending to have read this vivid philosophy into my most immediate impressions, and I may in fact perhaps not claim to have been really aware of its seed till a considerable time had passed, till apprehensions and reflections had taken place in quantity, immeasurable quantity, so to speak, and a great stir-up of the imagination been incurred. Undoubtedly is it in part the new—that is, more strictly, the elder—acuteness that I touch all the prime profit with; I didn't know at the time either how much appearances were all the while in the melting-pot or what wealth of reaction on them I was laying up. I cherish, for love of the unbroken interest, all the same, the theory of certain then positive and effective prefigurements, because it leaves me thus free for remarking that I knew where I was, as I may put it, from the moment I saw the state of the London to come brought down with the weight of her abdication of her genius. It not unnaturally may be said that it hasn't been till to-day that we *see* her genius in its fulness—throwing up in a hundred lights, matters we practically acknowledge, such a plastic side as we had never dreamed she possessed. The genius of accommodation is what we had last expected of her—accommodation to anything but her portentous self, for in *that* connection she was ever remarkable; and certainly the air of the generalised, the emulous smart modern capital has come to be written upon her larger and larger even while we look.

The unaccommodating and unaccommodated city remains none the less closely consecrated to one's fondest notion of her—the city too indifferent, too proud, too unaware, too stupid even if one will, to enter any lists that involved her moving from her base and that thereby, when one approached her from the alien *positive* places (I don't speak of the American, in those days too negative to be related at all) enjoyed the enormous "pull," for making her impression, of ignoring everything but her own perversities and then of driving these home with an emphasis not to be gainsaid. Since she didn't emulate, as I have termed it, so she practised her own arts altogether, and both these ways and these consequences were in the flattest opposition (*that* was the happy point!) to foreign felicities or foreign standards, so that the effect in every case was of the straightest reversal of them—with black for the foreign white and white for the foreign black, wet for the foreign dry and dry for the foreign wet, big for the foreign small and small for the foreign big: I needn't extend the catalogue. *Her* idiosyncrasy was never in the least to have been inferred or presumed; it could only, in general, make the outsider provisionally gape. She sat thus imperturbable in her felicities, and if that is how, remounting the stream of time, I like most to think of her, this is because if her interest is still undeniable—as that of overgrown things goes—it has yet lost its fineness of quality. Phenomena may be interesting, thank goodness, without being phenomena of elegant expression or of any other form of restless smartness, and when once type is strong, when once it plays up from deep sources, every show of its sincerity delivers us a message and we hang, to real suspense, on its continuance of energy, on its again and yet again consistently acquitting itself. So it keeps in tune, and, as the French adage says, *c'est le ton qui fait la chanson.* The mid-Victorian London was sincere—that was a vast virtue and a vast appeal; the contemporary is sceptical, and most so when most plausible; the turn of the tide could verily be fixed to an hour—the hour at which the new plausibility began to exceed the old sincerities by so much as a single sign. They could truly have been arrayed face to face, I think, for an attentive eye—and I risk even saying that my own, bent upon them, as was to come to pass, with a habit of anxiety that I should scarce be able to overstate, had its unrecorded penetrations, its alarms and recoveries, even perhaps its very lapses of faith, though always redeemed afresh by still fonder fanaticisms, to a pitch that shall perhaps present itself, when they expose it all the way, as that of tiresome extravagance. Exposing it all the way is none the less, I see, exactly what I plot against it—or, otherwise expressed, in favour of the fine truth of history, so far as a throb of that awful pulse has been matter of one's own life; in favour too of the mere returns derivable from more inordinate curiosity. These Notes would enjoy small self-respect, I think, if that principle, not to call it that passion, didn't almost furiously ride them.

III

I was at any rate in the midst of sincerities enough, sincerities of emphasis and "composition"; perversities, idiosyncrasies, incalculabilities, delightful all as densities at first insoluble, delightful even indeed as so much mere bewilderment and shock. When was the shock, I ask myself as I look back, not so deadened by the general atmospheric richness as not to melt more or less immediately into some succulence for the mind, something that could feed the historic sense almost to sweetness? I don't mean that it was a shock to be invited to breakfast—there were stronger ones than that; but was in fact the *trait de mœurs* that disconnected me with most rapidity and intensity from all I had left on the other side of the sea. To be so disconnected, for the time, and in the most insidious manner, was above all what I had come out for, and every appearance that might help it was to be artfully and gratefully cultivated. I recollect well how many of these combined as I sat at quite punctual fried sole and marmalade in the comparatively disengaged sitting-room of the second floor—the occupancy of the first has remained vague to me; disengaged from the mantle of gloom the folds of which draped most heavily the feet of the house, as it were, and thereby promoted in my own bower the chronic dusk favourable to mural decoration consisting mainly of framed and glazed "coloured" excisions from Christmas numbers of the Illustrated London News that had been at their hour quite modern miracles. Was it for that matter into a sudden splendour of the modern that ascendingly emerged under the hospitality of my kind fellow-tenant, or was it rather into the fine classicism of a bygone age, as literature and the arts had handed down that memory? Such were the questions whisked at every turn under my nose and reducing me by their obscure charm but to bewildered brooding, I fear, when I should have been myself, to repay these attentions, quite forward and informing and affirmative.

There were eminent gentlemen, as I was sure they could only be, to "meet" and, alas, awfully to interrogate me—for vivid has remained to me, as the best of my bewilderment, the strangeness of finding that I could be of interest to *them*: not indeed to call it rather the proved humiliation of my impotence. My identity for myself was *all* in my sensibility to their own exhibition, with not a scrap left over for a personal show; which made it as inconvenient as it was queer that I should be treated as a specimen and have in the most unexpected manner to prove that I was a good one. I knew myself the very worst conceivable, but how to give to such other persons a decent or coherent reason for my being so required more presence of mind than I could in the least muster—the consequence of which failure had to be for me, I fear, under all that confused first flush, rather an abject acceptance of the air of imbecility. There were, it appeared, things of interest taking place in America, and I had had, in this absurd manner, to come to England to learn it: I had had over there on the ground itself no conception of any such matter—nothing of the smallest interest, by any perception of mine, as I suppose I should still blush to recall, had taken place in America since the War. How *could* anything, I really wanted to ask—anything comparable, that is, to what was taking place under my eyes in Half-Moon Street and at dear softly presiding Rutson's table of talk. It doubtless essentially belonged to the exactly right type and tone and general figure of my fellow-breakfasters from the Temple, from the Home Office, the Foreign Office, the House of Commons, from goodness knew what other scarce discernible Olympian altitudes, it belonged to the very cut of their hair and their waistcoats and their whiskers—for it was still more or less a whiskered age—that they should desire from me much distinctness about General Grant's first cabinet, upon the formation of which the light of the newspaper happened then to beat; yet at the same time that I asked myself if it was to such cold communities, such flat frustrations as were so proposed, that I had sought to lift my head again in European air, I found the crisis enriched by sundry other apprehensions.

They melted together in it to that increase of savour I have already noted, yet leaving me vividly admonished that the blankness of my mind as to the Washington candidates relegated me to some class unencountered as yet by any one of my conversers, a class only not perfectly ridiculous because perfectly insignificant. Also that politics walked abroad in England, so that one might supremely bump against them, as much as, by my fond impression, they took their exercise in America but through the back streets and the ways otherwise untrodden and the very darkness of night; that further all lively attestations were *ipso facto* interesting, and that finally and in the supreme degree, the authenticity of whatever one was going to learn in the world would probably always have for its sign that one got it at some personal cost. To this generalisation mightn't one even add that in proportion as the cost was great, or became fairly excruciating, the lesson, the value acquired would probably be a thing to treasure? I remember really going so far as to wonder if any act of acquisition of the life-loving, life-searching sort that most appealed to me wouldn't mostly be fallacious if unaccompanied by that tag of the price paid in personal discomfort, in some self-exposure and some none too impossible consequent discomfiture, for the sake of it. Didn't I even on occasion mount to the very height of seeing it written that these bad moments were the downright consecration of knowledge, that is of perception and, essentially, of exploration, always dangerous and treacherous, and so might afterwards come to figure to memory, each in its order, as the silver nail on the wall of the temple where the trophy is hung up? All of which remark, I freely grant, is a great ado about the long since so bedimmed little Half-Moon Street breakfasts, and is moreover quite wide of the mark if suggesting that the joys of recognition, those of imaginatively, of projectively fitting in and fitting out every piece in the puzzle and every recruit to the force of a further understanding weren't in themselves a most bustling and cheering business.

It was bustling at least, assuredly, if not quite always in the same degree exhilarating, to breakfast out at all, as distinguished from lunching, without its being what the Harvard scene made of it, one of the incidents of "boarding"; it was association at a jump with the ghosts of Byron and Sheridan and Scott and Moore and Lockhart and Rogers and *tutti quanti*—as well as the exciting note of a social order in which everyone wasn't hurled straight, with the momentum of rising, upon an office or a store. The mere vision in numbers of persons embodying and in various ways sharply illustrating a clear alternative to that passivity told a tale that would be more and more worth the reading with every turn of the page. So at all events I fantasticated while harassed by my necessity to weave into my general tapestry every thread that would conduce to a pattern, and so the thread for instance of the great little difference of my literally never having but once "at home" been invited to breakfast on types as well as on toast and its accessories could suggest an effect of silk or silver when absolutely dangled before me. That single occasion at home came back in a light that fairly brought tears to my eyes, for it was touching now to the last wanness that the lady of the winter morn of the Massachusetts Sabbath, one of those, as I recover it, of 1868, to reach whose board we had waded through snowdrifts, had been herself fondling a reminiscence, though I can scarce imagine supposing herself to offer for our consumption any other type than her own. It was for that matter but the sweet staleness of her reminiscence that made her a type, and I remember how it had had to do thereby all the work: *she*, of an age to reach so considerably back, had breakfasted out, in London, and with Mr. Rogers himself—that was the point; which I am bound to say did for the hour and on that spot supply richness of reference enough. And I am caught up, I find, in the very act of this claim for my prior scantness of experience by a memory that makes it not a little less perfect and which is oddly enough again associated with a struggle, on an empty stomach, through the massed New England whiteness of the prime Sunday hour. I still cherish the vision, which couldn't then have faded from me, of my having, during the age of innocence—I mean of my own—breakfasted with W. D. Howells, insidious disturber and fertiliser of that state in me, to "meet" Bayard Taylor and Arthur Sedgwick all in the Venetian manner, the delightful Venetian manner which toward the later 'sixties draped any motion on our host's part as with a habit still appropriate. *He* had risen that morning under the momentum of his but recently concluded consular term in Venice, where margin, if only that of the great loungeable piazza, had a breadth, and though Sedgwick and I had rather, as it were, to take the jump standing, this was yet under the inspiration of feeling the case most special. Only it had *been* Venetian, snow-shoes and all; I had stored it sacredly away as not American at all, and was of course to learn in Half-Moon Street how little it had been English either.

What must have seemed to me of a fine international mixture, during those weeks, was my thrilling opportunity to sit one morning, beside Mrs. Charles Norton's tea-urn, in Queen's Gate Terrace, opposite to Frederic Harrison, eminent to me at the moment as one of the subjects of Matthew Arnold's early fine banter, one of his too confidently roaring "young lions" of the periodical press. Has any gilding ray since that happy season rested here and there with the sovereign charm of interest, of drollery, of felicity and infelicity taken on by scattered selected objects in that writer's bright critical dawn?—an element in which we had the sense of sitting gratefully bathed, so that we fairly took out our young minds and dabbled and soaked them in it as we were to do again in no other. The beauty was thus at such a rate that people had references, and that a reference was then, to my mind, whether in a person or an object, the most glittering, the most becoming ornament possible, a style of decoration one seemed likely to perceive figures here and there, whether animate or not, quite groan under the accumulation and the weight of. One had scarcely met it before—that I now understood; at the same time that there was perhaps a wan joy in one's never having missed it, by all appearance, having on the contrary ever instinctively caught it, on the least glimmer of its presence. Even when present, or what in the other time I had taken for present, it had been of the thinnest, whereas all about me hereafter it would be by all appearance almost glutinously thick—to the point even of one's on occasion sticking fast in it; that is finding intelligibility smothered in quantity. I lost breath in fact, no doubt, again and again, with this latter increase, but was to go on and on for a long time before any first glimmer of reaction against so special a source of interest. It attached itself to objects often, I saw, by no merit or virtue—above all, repeatedly, by no "cleverness"—of their own, but just by the luck of history, by the action of multiplicity of circumstance. Condemned the human particle "over here" was to *live* on whatever terms, in thickness—instead of being free, comparatively, or as I at once ruefully and exquisitely found myself, only to feel and to think in it. Ruefully because there were clearly a thousand contacts and sensations, of the strong direct order, that one lost by not so living; exquisitely because of the equal number of immunities and independences, blest independences of perception and judgment, blest liberties of range for the intellectual adventure, that accrued by the same stroke. These at least had the advantage, one of the most distinguished conceivable, that when enjoyed with a certain intensity they might produce the illusion of the other intensity, that of being involved in the composition and the picture itself, in the situations, the complications, the circumstances, admirable and dreadful; while no corresponding illusion, none making for the ideal play of reflection, conclusion, comparison, however one should incline to appraise the luxury, seemed likely to attend the immersed or engaged condition.

Whatever fatuity might at any rate have resided in these complacencies of view, I made them my own with the best conscience in the world, and I meet them again quite to extravagance of interest wherever on the whole extent of the scene my retrospect sets me down. It wasn't in the least at the same time that encountered celebrities only thus provoked the shifting play of my small lamp, and this too even though they were easily celebrated, by my measure, and though from the very first I owed an individual here and there among them, as was highly proper, the benefit of impression at the highest pitch. On the great supporting and enclosing scene itself, the big generalised picture, painted in layer upon layer and tone upon tone, one's fancy was all the while feeding; objects and items, illustrations and aspects might perpetually overlap or mutually interfere, but never without leaving consistency the more marked and character the more unmistakeable. The place, the places, bristled so for every glance with expressive particulars, that I really conversed with them, at happy moments, more than with the figures that moved in them, which affected me so often as but submissive articles of furniture, "put in" by an artist duly careful of effect and yet duly respectful of proportion. The great impression was doubtless no other then and there than what it is under every sky and before every scene that remind one afresh, at the given moment, of all the ways in which producing causes and produced creatures correspond and interdepend; but I think I must have believed at that time that these cross references kept up their game in the English air with a frankness and a good faith that kept the process, in all probability, the most traceable of its kind on the globe.

What was the secret of the force of that suggestion?—which was not, I may say, to be invalidated, to my eyes, by the further observation of cases and conditions. Was it that the enormous "pull" enjoyed at every point of the general surface the stoutness of the underlying belief in what was behind all surfaces?—so that the particular visible, audible, palpable fact, however small and subsidiary, was incomparably absolute, or had, so to speak, such

conscience and a confidence, such an absence of reserve and latent doubts
bout itself, as was not elsewhere to be found. Didn't such elements as that
present, in the heart of things, possibilities of scepticism, of mockery, of
ony, of the return of the matter, whatever it might be, on itself, by some
lay or other of the questioning spirit, the spirit therefore weakening to entire
omfort of affirmations? Didn't I see that humour itself, which might seem
lsewhere corrosive and subversive, was, as an English faculty, turned outward
ltogether and never turned inward?—by which convenient circumstance
ibversion, or in other words alteration and variation were not promoted.
uch truths were wondrous things to make out in such connections as my
xperience was then, and for no small time after, to be confined to; but I
ositively catch myself listening to them, even with my half-awakened ears,
s if they had been all so many sermons of the very stones of London. *There*,
> come back to it, was exactly the force with which these stones were to build
ne capaciously round: I invited them, I besought them, to say all they would,
nd—to return to my figure of a while back—it was soon so thoroughly
s if they had understood that, once having begun, they were to keep year
fter year fairly chattering to me. Many of these pages, I fondly foresee, must
onsist but of the record of their chatter. What was most of all happening, I
ake it, was that under an absurd special stress I was having, as who should say,
o improvise a local medium and to arrange a local consciousness. Against my
ue appropriation of those originally closest at my hand inevitable accidents
ad conspired—and, to conclude in respect to all this, if a considerable time
as to be wanted, in the event, for ideal certainty of adjustment, half the
erms required by this could then put forth the touching plea that they had
uite achingly waited.

IV

It may perhaps seem strange that the soil should have been watered by such an incident as Mr. Lazarus Fox's reply, in the earliest rich dusk, to my inquiry as to whither, while I occupied his rooms, I had best betake myself most regularly for my dinner: "Well, there is the Bath Hotel, sir, a very short walk away, where I should think you would be very comfortable indeed. Mr So-and-So dines at his club, sir—but there is also the Albany in Piccadilly to which I believe many gentlemen go." I think I measured on the spot "all that it took" to make my friend most advisedly—for it was clearly what he did—see me seated in lone state, for my evening meal, at the heavy mahogany of the stodgy little hotel that in those days and for long after occupied the north-west corner of Arlington Street and to which, in common with many compatriots, I repeatedly resorted during the years immediately following. We *suffered*, however, on those occasions, the unmitigated coffee-room of Mr Fox's prescription—it was part of a strange inevitability, a concomitant of necessary shelter and we hadn't at least gone forth to invoke its austere charm. I tried it, in that singular way, at the hour I speak of—and I well remember forecasting the interest of a social and moral order in which it could be supposed of me that, having tried it once, I should sublimely try it again. My success in doing so would indeed have been sublime, but a finer shade of the quality still attached somehow to my landlord's confidence in it; and this was one of the threads that, as I have called them, I was to tuck away for future picking-up again and unrolling. I fell back on the Albany, which long ago passed away and which I seem to have brushed with a touch of reminiscence in some anticipation of the present indulgence that is itself quite ancient history. It was a small eating-house of the very old English tradition, as I then supposed at least, just opposite the much greater establishment of the same name, which latter it had borrowed, and I remember wondering whether the tenants of the classic chambers, the beadle-guarded cluster of which was impressive even to the deprecated approach, found their conception of the "restaurant"—we still pronounced it in the French manner—met by the small compartments, narrow as horse-stalls, formed by the high straight backs of hard wooden benches and accommodating respectively two pairs of feeders, who were thus so closely face to face as fairly to threaten with knife and fork each others' more forward features.

The scene was sordid, the arrangements primitive, the detail of the procedure, as it struck me, well-nigh of the rudest; yet I remember rejoicing in it all—as one indeed might perfectly rejoice in the juiciness of joints and the abundance of accessory pudding; for I said to myself under every shock and at the hint of every savour that this was what it was for an exhibition to reek with local colour, and one could dispense with a napkin, with a crusty roll, with room for one's elbows or one's feet, with an immunity from intermittence of the "plain boiled," much better than one could dispense with that. There were restaurants galore even at that time in New York and in Boston, but I had never before had to do with an eating-house and had not yet seen the little old English world of Dickens, let alone of the ever-haunting Hogarth, of Smollett and of Boswell, drenched with such a flood of light. As one sat there one *understood*; one drew out the severe séance not to stay the assault of precious conspiring truths, not to break the current of in-rushing telltale suggestion. Every face was a documentary scrap, half a dozen broken words to piece with half a dozen others, and so on and on; every sound was strong, whether rich and fine or only queer and coarse; everything in this order drew a positive sweetness from never being—whatever else it was—gracelessly flat. The very rudeness was ripe, the very commonness was conscious—that is not related to mere other forms of the same, but to matters as different as possible, into which it shaded off and off or up and up; the image in fine was organic, rounded and complete, as definite as a Dutch picture of low life hung on a museum wall. "Low" I say in respect to the life; but that was the point for me, that whereas the smartness and newness beyond the sea supposedly disavowed the low, they did so but thinly and vainly, falling markedly short of the high; which the little boxed and boiled Albany attained to some effect of, after a fashion of its own, just by having its so thoroughly appreciable note-value in a scheme of manners. It was imbedded, so to speak, in the scheme, and it borrowed lights, it borrowed even glooms, from so much neighbouring distinction. The places across the sea, as they to my then eyes faintly after-glowed, had no impinging borders but those of the desert to borrow *from*. And if it be asked of me whether all the while I insist, for demonstration of the complacency with which I desire to revert, on not regretting the disappearance of such too long surviving sordidries as those I have evoked, I can but answer that blind emotion, in whichever sense directed, has nothing to say to the question and that the sense of what we just *could* confidently live by at a given far-away hour is a simple stout fact of relief.

Relief, again, I say, from the too enormous present accretions and alternatives—which we witlessly thought so innumerable then, which we artlessly found so much of the interest of *in* an immeasurable multiplicity and which I now feel myself thus grope for ghostly touch of in the name, neither more nor less, of poetic justice. I wasn't doubtless at the time so very sure, after all, of the comparative felicity of our state, that of the rare *moment* for the fond fancy—I doubtless even a bit greedily missed certain quantities, not to call them certain qualities, here and there, and the best of my actual purpose is to make amends for that blasphemy. There isn't a thing I can imagine having missed that I don't quite ache to miss again; and it remains at all events an odd stroke that, having of old most felt the thrill of the place in its mighty muchness, I have lived to adore it backward for its sweet simplicity. I find myself in fact at the present writing only too sorry when not able to minimise conscientiously this, that or the other of the old sources of impression. The thing is indeed admirably possible in a *general* way, though much of the exhibition was none the less undeniably, was absolutely large: how can I for instance recall the great cab-rank, mainly formed of delightful hansoms, that stretched along Piccadilly from the top of the Green Park unendingly down, without having to take it for unsurpassably modern and majestic? How can I think—I select my examples at hazard—of the "run" of the more successful of Mr. Robertson's comedies at the "dear little old" Prince of Wales's Theatre in Tottenham Court Road as anything less than one of the wonders of our age? How, by the same token, can I not lose myself still more in the glory of a time that was to watch the drawn-out procession of Henry Irving's Shakespearean splendours at the transcendent Lyceum? or how, in the same general line, not recognise that to live through the extravagant youth of the æsthetic era, whether as embodied in the then apparently inexhaustible vein of the Gilbert and Sullivan operas or as more monotonously expressed in those "last words" of the *raffiné* that were chanted and crooned in the damask-hung temple of the Grosvenor Gallery, was to seem privileged to such immensities as history would find left to her to record but with bated breath?

These latter triumphs of taste, however, though lost in the abysm now, had then a good many years to wait and I alight for illustrative support of my present mild thesis on the comparative humility, say, of the inward aspects, in a large measure, of the old National Gallery, where memory mixes for me together so many elements of the sense of an antique world. The great element was of course that I well-nigh incredibly stood again in the immediate presence of Titian and Rembrandt, of Rubens and Paul Veronese, and that the cup of sensation was thereby filled to overflowing; but I look at it to-day as concomitantly warm and closed-in and, as who should say, cosy that the ancient order and contracted state and thick-coloured dimness, all unconscious of rearrangements and reversals, blighting new lights and invidious shattering comparisons, still prevailed and kept contemplation comfortably confused and serenely superstitious, when not indeed at its sharpest moments quite fevered with incoherences. The place looks to me across the half century richly dim, yet at the same time both perversely plain and heavily violent—violent through indifference to the separations and selections that have become a tribute to modern nerves; but I cherish exactly those facts of benightedness, seeming as they do to have positively and blessedly conditioned the particular sweetness of wonder with which I haunted the Family of Darius, the Bacchus and Ariadne, or the so-called portrait of Ariosto. Could one in those days feel anything with force, whether for pleasure or for pain, without feeling it as an immense little act or event of life, and as therefore taking place on a scene and in circumstances scarce at all to be separated from its own sense and impact?—so that to recover it is to recover the whole medium, the material pressure of things, and find it most marked for preservation as an aspect, even, distinguishably, a "composition."

What a composition, for instance again I am capable at this hour of exclaiming, the conditions of felicity in which I became aware, one afternoon during a renewed gape before the Bacchus and Ariadne, first that a little gentleman beside me and talking with the greatest vivacity to another gentleman was extremely remarkable, second that he had the largest and most *chevelu* auburn head I had ever seen perched on a scarce perceptible body, third that I held some scrap of a clue to his identity, which couldn't fail to be eminent, fourth that this tag of association was with nothing less than a small photograph sent me westward across the sea a few months before, and fifth that the sitter for the photograph had been the author of Atalanta in Calydon and Poems and Ballads! I thrilled, it perfectly comes back to me, with the prodigy of this circumstance that I should be admiring Titian in the same breath with Mr. Swinburne—that is in the same breath in which *he* admired Titian and in which I also admired *him*, the whole constituting on the spot between us, for appreciation, that is for mine, a fact of intercourse, such a fact as could stamp and colour the whole passage ineffaceably, and this even though the more illustrious party to it had within the minute turned off and left me shaken. I was shaken, but I was satisfied—that was the point; I didn't ask more to interweave another touch in my pattern, and as I once more gather in the impression I am struck with my having deserved truly as many of the like as possible. I was welcome to them, it may well be said, on such easy terms—and yet I ask myself whether, after all, it didn't take on my own part some doing, as we nowadays say, to make them so well worth having. They themselves took, I even at the time felt, little enough trouble for it, and the virtue of the business was repeatedly, no doubt, a good deal more in what I brought than in what I took.

I apply this remark indeed to those extractions of the quintessence that had for their occasion either one's more undirected though never fruitless walks and wanderings or one's earnest, one's positively pious approach to whatever consecrated ground or shrine of pilgrimage that might be at the moment in order. There was not a regular prescribed "sight" that I during those weeks neglected—I remember haunting the museums in especial, though the South Kensington was then scarce more than embryonic, with a sense of duty and of excitement that I was never again to know combined in equal measure, I think, and that it might really have taken some element of personal danger to account for. There *was* the element, in a manner, to ason the cup with sharpness—the danger, all the while, that my freedom light be brief and my experience broken, that I was under the menace of ncertainty and subject in fine to interruption. The fact of having been so ong gravely unwell sufficed by itself to keep apprehension alive; it was our lea, or at least quite intensely mine, that what I was doing, could I but put through, would be intimately good for me—only the putting it through as the difficulty, and I sometimes faltered by the way. This makes now for general air on the part of all the objects of vision that I recover, and almost s much in those of accidental encounter as in the breathlessly invoked, of eing looked at for the last time and giving out their message and story as ith the still, collected passion of an only chance. This feeling about them, ot to say, as I might have imputed it, *in* them, wonderfully helped, as may be elieved, the extraction of quintessences—which sprang at me of themselves, r that matter, out of any appearance that confessed to the least value in the ompound, the least office in the harmony. If the commonest street-vista as a fairly heart-shaking contributive image, if the incidents of the thick nascent light anywhere, and the perpetual excitement of never knowing, etween it and the historic and determined gloom, which was which and hich one would most "back" for the general outcome and picture, so the reat sought-out compositions, the Hampton Courts and the Windsors, the ichmonds, the Dulwiches, even the very Hampstead Heaths and Putney ommons, to say nothing of the Towers, the Temples, the Cathedrals and le strange penetrabilities of the City, ranged themselves like the rows of great gures in a sum, an amount immeasurably huge, that one would draw on if ot quite as long as one lived, yet as soon as ever one should seriously get to ork. That, to a tune of the most beautiful melancholy—at least as I catch again now—was the way all values came out: they were charged somehow ith a useability the most immediate, the most urgent, and which, I seemed o see, would keep me restless till I should have done something of my very wn with them.

This was indeed perhaps what most painted them over with the dmonitory appeal: there were truly moments at which they seemed not to nswer for it that I should get all the good of them, and the finest—what I as so extravagantly, so fantastically after—unless I could somehow at once indite my sonnet and prove my title. The difficulty was all in there being so much of them—I might myself have been less restless if they could only have been less vivid. This they absolutely declined at any moment and in any connection to be, and it was ever so long till they abated a jot of the refusal. Thereby, in consequence, as may easily be judged, they were to keep me in alarms to which my measures practically taken, my catastrophes anxiously averted, remained not quite proportionate. I recall a most interesting young man who had been my shipmate on the homeward-bound "China," shortly before—I could go at length into my reasons for having been so struck with him, but I forbear—who, on our talking, to my intense trepidation of curiosity, of where I might advisedly "go" in London, let me know that he always went to Craven Street Strand, where bachelor lodgings were highly convenient, and whence I in fact then saw them flush at me over the cold grey sea with an authenticity almost fierce. I didn't in the event, as has been seen, go to Craven Street for rooms, but I did go, on the very first occasion, for atmosphere, neither more nor less—the young man of the ship, building so much better than he knew, had guaranteed me such a rightness of that and it belongs to this reminiscence, for the triviality of which I should apologize did I find myself at my present pitch capable of apologizing for anything, that I had on the very spot there one of those hallucinations a to the precious effect dreadful to lose and yet impossible to render which interfused the æsthetic dream in presence of its subject with the mortal drop of despair (as I should insist at least didn't the despair itself seem to have acted here as the preservative). The precious effect in the case of Craven Street was that it absolutely reeked, to my fond fancy, with associations born of the particular ancient piety embodied in one's private altar to Dickens; and that this upstart little truth alone would revel in explanations that I should for the time have feverishly to forego. The exquisite matter was not the identification with the scene of special shades or names; it was just that the whole Dickens procession marched up and down, the whole Dickens world looked out of its queer, quite sinister windows—for it was the socially sinister Dickens, I am afraid, rather than the socially encouraging or confoundingly comic who still at that moment was most apt to meet me with his reasons. Such a reason was just that look of the inscrutable riverward street, packed to blackness with accumulations of suffered experience, these, indescribably, disavowed and confessed at one and the same time, and with the fact of its blocked old Thames-side termination, a mere fact of more oppressive enclosure now, telling all sorts of vague loose stories about it.

V

Why, however, should I pick up so small a crumb from that mere brief first course at a banquet of initiation which was in the event to prolong itself through years and years?—unless indeed as a scrap of a specimen, chosen at hazard, of the prompt activity of a process by which my intelligence afterwards came to find itself more fed, I think, than from any other source at all, or, for that matter, from all other sources put together. A hundred more suchlike modest memories breathe upon me, each with its own dim little plea, as I turn to face them, but my idea is to deal somehow more conveniently with the whole gathered mass of my subsequent impressions in this order, a fruitage that I feel to have been only too abundantly stored. Half a dozen of those of a larger and more immediate dignity, incidents more particularly of the rather invidiously so-called social contact, pull my sleeve as I pass; but the long, backward-drawn train of the later life drags them along with it, lost and smothered in its spread—only one of them stands out or remains over, insisting on its place and hour, its felt distinguishability. To this day I feel again *that* roused emotion, my unsurpassably prized admission to the presence of the great George Eliot, whom I was taken to see, by one of the kind door-opening Norton ladies, by whom Mrs. Lewes's guarded portal at North Bank appeared especially penetrable, on a Sunday afternoon of April '69. Later occasions, after a considerable lapse, were not to overlay the absolute face-value, as I may call it, of all the appearances then and there presented me—which were taken home by a young spirit almost abjectly grateful, at any rate all devoutly prepared, for them. I find it idle even to wonder what "place" the author of Silas Marner and Middlemarch may be conceived to have in the pride of our literature—so settled and consecrated in the individual range of view is many such a case free at last to find itself, free after ups and downs, after fluctuations of fame or whatever, which have divested judgment of any relevance that isn't most of all the relevance of a living and recorded *relation*. It has ceased then to know itself in any degree as an estimate, has shaken off the anxieties of circumspection and comparison and just grown happy to act as an attachment pure and simple, an effect of life's own logic, but in the ashes of which the wonted fires of youth need but to be blown upon for betrayal of a glow. Reflective appreciation may have originally been concerned, whether at its most or at its least, but it is well over, to our infinite relief—yes, to our immortal comfort, I think; the interval back cannot again be bridged. We simply sit with our enjoyed gain, our residual rounded possession in our lap; a safe old treasure, which has ceased to shrink, if indeed also perhaps greatly to swell, and all that further touches it is the fine vibration set up if the name we know it all by is called into question—perhaps however little.

It was by George Eliot's name that I was to go on knowing, was never to cease to know, a great treasure of beauty and humanity, of applied and achieved art, a testimony, historic as well as æsthetic, to the deeper interest of the intricate English aspects; and I now allow the vibration, as I have called it, all its play—quite as if I had been wronged even by my own hesitation as to whether to pick up my anecdote. That scruple wholly fades with the sense of how I must at the very time have foreseen that here was one of those associations that would determine in the far future an exquisite inability to revise it. Middlemarch had not then appeared—we of the faith were still to enjoy that saturation, and Felix Holt the radical was upwards of three years old; the impetus proceeding from this work, however, was still fresh enough in my pulses to have quickened the palpitation of my finding myself in presence. I had rejoiced without reserve in Felix Holt—the illusion of reading which, outstretched on my then too frequently inevitable bed at Swampscott during a couple of very hot days of the summer of 1866, comes back to me, followed by that in sooth of sitting up again, at no great ease, to indite with all promptness a review of the delightful thing, the place of appearance of which nothing could now induce me to name, shameless about the general fact as I may have been at the hour itself: over such a feast of fine rich natural tone did I feel myself earnestly bend. Quite unforgettable to me the art and truth with which the note of this tone was struck in the beautiful prologue and the bygone appearances, a hundred of the outward and visible signs of the author's own young rural and midmost England, made to hold us by their harmony. The book was not, if I rightly remember, altogether genially greeted, but I was to hold fast to the charm I had thankfully suffered it, I had been conscious of absolutely needing it, to work.

43

Exquisite the remembrance of how it wouldn't have "done" for me at all, in relation to other inward matters, not to strain from the case the last drop of its happiest sense. And I had even with the cooling of the first glow so little gone back upon it, as we have nowadays learned to say, had in fact so gone forward, floated by its wave of superlative intended benignity, that, once in the cool quiet drawing-room at North Bank I knew myself steeped in still deeper depths of the medium. G. H. Lewes was absent for the time on an urgent errand; one of his sons, on a visit at the house, had been suddenly taken with a violent attack of pain, the heritage of a bad accident not long before in the West Indies, a suffered onset from an angry bull, I seem to recall, who had tossed or otherwise mauled him, and, though beaten off, left him considerably compromised—these facts being promptly imparted to us, in no small flutter, by our distinguished lady, who came in to us from another room, where she had been with the hapless young man while his father appealed to the nearest good chemist for some known specific. It infinitely moved me to see so great a celebrity quite humanly and familiarly agitated— even with something clear and noble in it too, to which, as well as to the extraordinarily interesting dignity of her whole odd personal conformation, I remember thinking her black silk dress and the lace mantilla attached to her head and keeping company on either side with the low-falling thickness of her dark hair effectively contributed. I have found myself, my life long, attaching value to every noted thing in respect to a great person—and George Eliot struck me on the spot as somehow *illustratively* great; never at any rate has the impression of those troubled moments faded from me, nor that at once of a certain high grace in her anxiety and a frank immediate appreciation of our presence, modest embarrassed folk as we were. It took me no long time to thrill with the sense, sublime in its unexpectedness, that we were perhaps, or indeed quite clearly, helping her to pass the time till Mr. Lewes's return—after which he would again post off for Mr. Paget the pre-eminent surgeon; and I see involved with this the perfect amenity of her assisting us, as it were, to assist her, through unrelinquished proper talk, due responsible remark and report, in the last degree suggestive to me, on a short holiday taken with Mr. Lewes in the south of France, whence they had just returned. Yes indeed, the lightest words of great persons are so little as any words of others are

1at I catch myself again inordinately struck with her dropping it off-hand 1at the mistral, scourge of their excursion, had blown them into Avignon, here they had gone, I think, to see J. S. Mill, only to blow them straight ut again—the figure put it so before us; as well as with the moral interest, 1e absence of the *banal*, in their having, on the whole scene, found pleasure 1rther poisoned by the frequency in all those parts of "evil faces: oh the evil 1ces!" *That* recorded source of suffering enormously affected me—I felt it as eautifully characteristic: I had never heard an *impression de voyage* so little 1inted with the superficial or the vulgar. I was myself at the time in the thick f impressions, and it was true that they would have seemed to me rather to 1il of life, of their own doubtless inferior kind, if submitting beyond a certain oint to be touched with that sad or, as who should say, that grey colour: 1rs. Lewes's were, it appeared, predominantly so touched, and I could at 1nce admire it in them and wonder if they didn't pay for this by some lack of 1tensity on other sides. Why I didn't more impute to her, or to them, that ossible lack is more than I can say, since under the law of moral earnestness 1e vulgar and the trivial would be then involved in the poor observations of 1y own making—a conclusion sufficiently depressing.

However, I didn't find myself depressed, and I didn't find the great mind 1at was so good as to shine upon us at that awkward moment however dimly 1nything but augmented; what was its sensibility to the evil faces but part of 1e large old tenderness which the occasion had caused to overflow and on 'hich we were presently floated back into the room she had left?—where we 1ight perhaps beguile a little the impatience of the sufferer waiting for relief. Ve ventured in our flutter to doubt whether we *should* beguile, we held back ʌith a certain delicacy from this irruption, and if there was a momentary ʌonderful and beautiful conflict I remember how our yielding struck me as rowned with the finest grace it could possibly have, that of the prodigious rivilege of humouring, yes literally humouring so renowned a spirit at a 1oment when we could really match our judgment with hers. For the injured 'oung man, in the other and the larger room, simply lay stretched on his back 1 the floor, the posture apparently least painful to him—though painful 1nough at the best I easily saw on kneeling beside him, after my first dismay, ɔ ask if I could in any way ease him. I see his face again, fair and young and

flushed, with its vague little smile and its moist brow; I recover the momen
or two during which we sought to make natural conversation in his presence
and my question as to what conversation *was* natural; and then as his father'
return still failed my having the inspiration that at once terminated the strair
of the scene and yet prolonged the sublime connection. Mightn't *I* then hurry
off for Mr. Paget?—on whom, as fast as a cab could carry me, I would wai
with the request that he would come at the first possible moment to the
rescue. Mrs. Lewes's and our stricken companion's instant appreciation o
this offer lent me wings on which I again feel myself borne very much a
if suddenly acting as a messenger of the gods—surely I had never come so
near to performing in that character. I shook off my fellow visitor for swifte
cleaving of the air, and I recall still feeling that I cleft it even in the dull four-
wheeler of other days which, on getting out of the house, I recognised as the
only object animating, at a distance, the long blank Sunday vista beside the
walled-out Regent's Park. I crawled to Hanover Square—or was it Cavendish
I let the question stand—and, after learning at the great man's door tha
though he was not at home he was soon expected back and would receive my
message without delay, cherished for the rest of the day the particular quality
of my vibration.

It was doubtless even excessive in proportion to its cause—yet in what
else but that consisted the force and the use of vibrations? It was by their exces
that one knew them for such, as one for that matter only knew things in genera
worth knowing. I didn't know what I had expected as an effect of our offered
homage, but I had somehow not, at the best, expected a relation—and now a
relation had been dramatically determined. It would exist for me if I should
never again in all the world ask a feather's weight of it; for myself, that is, it
would simply never be able not somehow to act. Its virtue was not in truth
at all flagrantly to be put to the proof—any opportunity for that underwent
at the best a considerable lapse; but why wasn't it intensely acting, none the
less, during the time when, before being in London again for any length of
stay, I found it intimately concerned in my perusal of Middlemarch, so soon
then to appear, and even in that of Deronda, its intervention on behalf of
which defied any chill of time? And to these references I can but subjoin that
they obviously most illustrate the operation of a sense for drama. The process

of appropriation of the two fictions was experience, in great intensity, and roundabout the field was drawn the distinguishable ring of something that belonged equally to this condition and that embraced and further vivified the imaged mass, playing in upon it lights of surpassing fineness. So it was, at any rate, that my "relation"—for I didn't go so far as to call it "ours"—helped me to squeeze further values from the intrinsic substance of the copious final productions I have named, a weight of variety, dignity and beauty of which I have never allowed my measure to shrink.

Even this example of a rage for connections, I may also remark, doesn't deter me from the mention here, somewhat out of its order of time, of another of those in which my whole privilege of reference to Mrs. Lewes, such as it remained, was to look to be preserved. I stretch over the years a little to overtake it, and it calls up at once another person, the ornament, or at least the diversion, of a society long since extinct to me, but who, in common with every bearer of a name I yield to the temptation of writing, insists on profiting promptly by the fact of inscription—very much as if first tricking me into it and then proving it upon me. The extinct societies that once were so sure of themselves, how can they *not* stir again if the right touch, that of a hand they actually knew, however little they may have happened to heed it, reaches tenderly back to them? The touch *is* the retrieval, so far as it goes, setting up as it does heaven knows what undefeated continuity. I must have been present among the faithful at North Bank during a Sunday afternoon or two of the winter of '77 and '78—I was to see the great lady alone but on a single occasion before her death; but those attestations are all but lost to me now in the livelier pitch of a scene, as I can only call it, of which I feel myself again, all amusedly, rather as sacrificed witness. I had driven over with Mrs. Greville from Milford Cottage, in Surrey, to the villa George Eliot and George Lewes had not long before built themselves, and which they much inhabited, at Witley—this indeed, I well remember, in no great flush of assurance that my own measure of our intended felicity would be quite that of my buoyant hostess. But here exactly comes, with my memory of Mrs. Greville, from which numberless by-memories dangle, the interesting question that makes for my recall why things happened, under her much-waved wing, not in any too coherent fashion—and this even though it was never once given her, I surmise, to guess that they anywhere fell short. So gently used, all round indeed, was this large, elegant, extremely near-sighted and extremely demonstrative lady, whose genius was all for friendship, admiration, declamation and expenditure, that one doubted whether in the whole course of her career she had ever once been brought up, as it were, against a recognised reality; other at least perhaps than the tiresome cost of the materially agreeable in life and the perverse appearance, at times, that though she "said" things, otherwise recited choice morceaux, whether French or English, with a marked oddity of manner, of "attack," a general incongruity of drawing-room art, the various contributive elements, hour, scene, persuaded patience and hushed attention, were perforce a precarious quantity.

It is in that bygone old grace of the unexploded factitious, the air of a thousand dimmed illusions and more or less early Victorian beatitudes on the part of the blandly idle and the supposedly accomplished, that Mrs. Greville, with her exquisite good-nature and her innocent fatuity, is embalmed for me; so that she becomes in that light a truly shining specimen, almost the image or compendium of a whole side of a social order. Just so she has happy suggestion; just so, whether or no by a twist of my mind toward the enviability of certain complacencies of faith and taste that we would yet neither live back into if we could, nor can catch again if we would. I see my forgotten friend of that moist autumn afternoon of our call, and of another, on the morrow, which I shall not pass over, as having rustled and gushed and protested and performed through her term under a kind of protection by the easy-going gods that is not of this fierce age. Amiabilities and absurdities, harmless serenities and vanities, pretensions and undertakings unashamed, still profited by the mildness of the critical air and the benignity of the social—on the right side at least of the social line. It had struck me from the first that nowhere so much as in England was it fortunate to *be* fortunate, and that against that condition, once it had somehow been handed down and determined, a number of the sharp truths that one might privately apprehend beat themselves beautifully in vain. I say beautifully for I confess without scruple to have found again and again at that time an attaching charm in the general exhibition of enjoyed immunity, paid for as it was almost always by the personal amenity, the practice of all sorts of pleasantness; if it kept the gods themselves for the time in good-humour, one was willing enough, or at least I was, to be on the side of the gods. Unmistakable too, as I seem to recover it, was the positive interest of watching and noting, roundabout one, for the turn, or rather for the blest continuity, of their benevolence: such an appeal proceeded, in this, that and the other particular case, from the fool's paradise really rounded and preserved, before one's eyes, for those who were so good as to animate it. There was always the question of how long they would be left to, and the growth of one's fine suspense, not to say one's frank little gratitude, as the miracle repeated itself.

All of which, I admit, dresses in many reflections the small circumstance that Milford Cottage, with its innumerable red candles and candle-shades, had affected me as the most embowered retreat for social innocence that it was possible to conceive, and as absolutely settling the question of whether the practice of pleasantness mightn't quite ideally pay for the fantastic protectedness. The red candles in the red shades have remained with me, inexplicably, as a vivid note of this pitch, shedding their rosy light, with the autumn gale, the averted reality, all shut out, upon such felicities of feminine helplessness as I couldn't have prefigured in advance and as exemplified, for further gathering in, the possibilities of the old tone. Nowhere had the evening curtains seemed so drawn, nowhere the copious service so soft, nowhere the second volume of the new novel, "half-uncut," so close to one's hand, nowhere the exquisite head and incomparable brush of the domesticated collie such an attestation of *that* standard at least, nowhere the harmonies of accident—of intention was more than one could say—so incapable of a wrong deflection. That society would lack the highest finish without some such distributed clusters of the thoroughly gentle, the mildly presumptuous and the inveterately mistaken, was brought home to me there, in fine, to a tune with which I had no quarrel, perverse enough as I had been from an early time to know but the impulse to egg on society to the fullest discharge of any material stirring within its breast and not making for cruelty or brutality, mere baseness or mere stupidity, that would fall into a picture or a scene. The quality of serene anxiety on the part for instance of exquisite Mrs. Thellusson, Mrs. Greville's mother, was by itself a plea for any privilege one should fancy her perched upon; and I scarce know if this be more or be less true because the anxiety—at least as I culled its fragrance—was all about the most secondary and superfluous small matters alone. It struck me, I remember, as a new and unexpected form of the pathetic altogether; and there was no form of the pathetic, any more than of the tragic or the comic, that didn't serve as another pearl for one's lengthening string. And I pass over what was doubtless the happiest stroke in the composition, the fact of its involving, as all-distinguished husband of the other daughter, an illustrious soldier and servant of his sovereign, of his sovereigns that were successively to be, than against whose patient handsome bearded presence the whole complexus of femininities and futilities couldn't have been left in more tolerated and more contrasted relief; pass it over to remind myself of how, in my particular friend of the three, the comic and the tragic were presented in a confusion that made the least intended of them at any moment take effectively the place of the most. The impression, that is, was never that of the sentiment operating—save indeed perhaps when the dear lady applied her faculty for frank imitation of the ridiculous, which she then quite directly and remarkably achieved; but that she could be comic, that she *was* comic, was what least appeased her unrest, and there were reasons enough, in a word, why her failure of the grand manner or the penetrating note should evoke the idea of their opposites perfectly achieved. She sat, alike in adoration and emulation, at the feet of my admirable old friend Fanny Kemble, the good-nature of whose consent to "hear" her was equalled only by the immediately consequent action of the splendidly corrective spring on the part of that unsurpassed subject of the dramatic afflatus fairly, or, as I should perhaps above all say, contradictiously provoked. Then aspirant and auditor, rash adventurer and shy alarmist, were swept away together in the gust of magnificent rightness and beauty, no scrap of the far-scattered prime proposal being left to pick up.

Which detail of reminiscence has again stayed my course to the Witley Villa, when even on the way I quaked a little with my sense of what *generally* most awaited or overtook my companion's prime proposals. What had come most to characterise the Leweses to my apprehension was that there couldn't be a thing in the world about which they weren't, and on the most conceded and assured grounds, almost scientifically particular; which presumption, however, only added to the relevance of one's learning

ow such a matter as their relation with Mrs. Greville could in accordance
with noble consistencies be carried on. I could trust *her* for it perfectly, as she
knew no law but that of innocent and exquisite aberration, never wanting
and never less than consecrating, and I fear I but took refuge for the rest in
declining all responsibility. I remember trying to say to myself that, even such
as we were, our visit couldn't but scatter a little the weight of cloud on the
Olympus we scaled—given the dreadful drenching afternoon we were after
all an imaginable short solace there; and this indeed would have borne me
through to the end save for an incident which, with a quite ideal logic, left
our adventure an approved ruin. I see again our bland, benign, commiserating
hostess beside the fire in a chill desert of a room where the master of the house
guarded the opposite hearthstone, and I catch once more the impression of no
occurrence of anything at all appreciable but their liking us to have come, with
our terribly trivial contribution, mainly from a prevision of how they should
more devoutly like it when we departed. It is remarkable, but the occasion
yields me no single echo of a remark on the part of any of us—nothing more
than the sense that our great author herself peculiarly suffered from the fury
of the elements, and that they had about them rather the minimum of the
paraphernalia of reading and writing, not to speak of that of tea, a conceivable
feature of the hour, but which was not provided for. Again I felt touched with
privilege, but not, as in '69, with a form of it redeemed from barrenness by
a motion of my own, and the taste of barrenness was in fact in my mouth
under the effect of our taking leave. We did so with considerable flourish till
we had passed out to the hall again, indeed to the door of the waiting carriage,
toward which G. H. Lewes himself all sociably, *then* above all conversingly,
wafted us—yet staying me by a sudden remembrance before I had entered
the brougham and signing me to wait while he repaired his omission. I
returned to the doorstep, whence I still see him reissue from the room we
had just left and hurry toward me across the hall shaking high the pair of
blue-bound volumes his allusion to the uninvited, the verily importunate
loan of which by Mrs. Greville had lingered on the air after his dash in quest
of them; "Ah those books—take them away, please, away, away!" I hear him
unreservedly plead while he thrusts them again at me, and I scurry back into
our conveyance, where, and where only, settled afresh with my companion,

I venture to assure myself of the horrid truth that had squinted at me as relieved our good friend of his superfluity. What indeed was this superfluity but the two volumes of my own precious "last"—we were still in the blest age of volumes—presented by its author to the lady of Milford Cottage, and by her, misguided votary, dropped with the best conscience in the world into the Witley abyss, out of which it had jumped with violence, under the touch of accident, straight up again into my own exposed face?

The bruise inflicted there I remember feeling for the moment only as sharp, such a mixture of delightful small questions at once salved it over and such a charm in particular for me to my recognising that this particular wrong—inflicted all unawares, which exactly made it sublime—was the only rightness of our visit. Our hosts hadn't so much as connected book with author, or author with visitor, or visitor with anything but the convenience of his ridding them of an unconsidered trifle; grudging as they so justifiedly did the impingement of such matters on their consciousness. The vivid demonstration of one's failure to penetrate there had been in the sweep of Lewes's gesture, which could scarce have been bettered by his actually wielding a broom. I think nothing passed between us in the brougham on revelation of the identity of the offered treat so emphatically declined—I see that I couldn't have laughed at it to the confusion of my gentle neighbour. But I quite recall my grasp of the *interest* of our distinguished friends' inaccessibility to the unattended plea, with the light it seemed to throw on what it was really to *be* attended. Never, never save as attended—by presumptions, that is, far other than any then hanging about one—would one so much as desire *not* to be pushed out of sight. I needn't attempt, however, to supply all the links in the chain of association which led to my finally just qualified beatitude: I had been served right enough in all conscience, but the pity was that Mrs. Greville had been. This I never wanted for her; and I may add, in the connection, that I discover now no grain of false humility in my having enjoyed in my own person adorning such a tale. There was positively a fine high thrill in thinking of persons—or at least of a person, for any fact about Lewes was but derivative—engaged in my own pursuit and yet detached, by what I conceived, detached by a pitch of intellectual life, from all that made it actual to myself. *There* was the lift of contemplation, there the inspiring image and the big supporting truth; the pitch of intellectual life in the very fact of which we seemed, my hostess and I, to have caught our celebrities sitting in that queer bleak way wouldn't have bullied me in the least if it hadn't been the centre of such a circle of gorgeous creation. It was the fashion among the profane in short either to misdoubt, before George Eliot's canvas, the latter's backing of rich thought, or else to hold that this matter of philosophy, and even if but of the philosophic vocabulary, thrust itself through to the confounding of the picture. But with that thin criticism I wasn't, as I have already intimated, to have a moment's patience; I was to become, I was to remain—I take pleasure in repeating—even a very Derondist of Derondists, for my own wanton joy: which amounts to saying that I found the figured, coloured tapestry *always* vivid enough to brave no matter what complication of the stitch.

VI

I take courage to confess moreover that I am carried further still by the current on which Mrs. Greville, friend of the super-eminent, happens to have launched me; for I can neither forbear a glance at one or two of the other adventures promoted by her, nor in the least dissociate her from that long aftertaste of them, such as they were, which I have positively cultivated. I ask myself first, however, whether or no our drive to Aldworth, on the noble height of Blackdown, had been preceded by the couple of occasions in London on which I was to feel I saw the Laureate most at his ease, yet on reflection concluding that the first of these—and the fewest days must have separated them—formed my prime introduction to the poet I had earliest known and best loved. The revelational evening I speak of is peopled, to my memory, not a little, yet with a confusedness out of which Tennyson's own presence doesn't at all distinctly emerge; he was occupying a house in Eaton Place, as appeared then his wont, for the earlier weeks of the spring, and I seem to recover that I had "gone on" to it, after dining somewhere else, under protection of my supremely kind old friend the late Lord Houghton, to whom I was indebted in those years for a most promiscuous befriending. He must have been of the party, and Mrs. Greville quite independently must, since I catch again the vision of her, so expansively and voluminously seated that she might fairly have been couchant, so to say, for the proposed characteristic act—there was a deliberation about it that precluded the idea of a spring; that, namely, of addressing something of the Laureate's very own to the Laureate's very face. Beyond the sense that he took these things with a gruff philosophy—and could always repay them, on the spot, in heavily-shovelled coin of the same mint, since it *was* a question of his genius—I gather in again no determined impression, unless it may have been, as could only be probable, the effect of fond prefigurements utterly blighted.

The fond prefigurements of youthful piety are predestined more often than not, I think, experience interfering, to strange and violent shocks; from which no general appeal is conceivable save by the prompt preclusion either of faith or of knowledge, a sad choice at the best. No other such illustration recurs to me of the possible refusal of those two conditions of an acquaintance to recognise each other at a given hour as the silent crash of which I was to be conscious several years later, in Paris, when placed in presence of M. Ernest Renan, from the surpassing distinction of whose literary face, with its exquisite finish of every feature, I had from far back extracted every sort of shining gage, a presumption general and positive. Widely enough to sink all interest—that was the dreadful thing—opened there the chasm between the implied, as I had taken it, and the attested, as I had, at the first blush, to take it; so that one was in fact scarce to know what might have happened if interest hadn't by good fortune already reached such a compass as to stick half way down the descent. What interest *can* survive becomes thus, surely, as much one of the lessons of life as the number of ways in which it remains impossible. What comes up in face of the shocks, as I have called them, is the question of a shift of every supposition, a change of base under fire, as it were; which must take place successfully if one's advance be not abandoned altogether. I remember that I saw the Tennyson directly presented as just utterly other than the Tennyson indirectly, and if the readjustment, for acquaintance, was less difficult than it was to prove in the case of the realised Renan the obligation to accept the difference—wholly as difference and without reference to strict loss or gain—was like a rap on the knuckles of a sweet superstition. Fine, fine, fine could he only be—fine in the sense of that quality in the texture of his verse, which had appealed all along by its most inward principle to one's taste, and had by the same stroke shown with what a force of lyric energy and sincerity the kind of beauty so engaged for could be associated. Was it that I had preconceived him in that light as pale and penetrating, as emphasising in every aspect the fact that he was fastidious? was it that I had supposed him more fastidious than really *could* have been— at the best for that effect? was it that the grace of the man *couldn't*, by my measure, but march somehow with the grace of the poet, given a perfection of this grace? was it in fine that style of a particular kind, when so highly developed, seemed logically to leave no room for other quite contradictious kinds? These were considerations of which I recall the pressure, at the same time that I fear I have no account of them to give after they have fairly faced the full, the monstrous demonstration that Tennyson was not Tennysonian. The desperate sequel to that was that he thereby changed one's own state too, one's beguiled, one's æsthetic; for what *could* this strange apprehension do but reduce the Tennysonian amount altogether? It dried up, to a certain extent, that is, in my own vessel of sympathy—leaving me so to ask whether it was before or after that I should take myself for the bigger fool. There had been folly somewhere; yet let me add that once I recognised this, once I felt the old fond pitch drop of itself, not alone inevitably, but very soon quite conveniently and while I magnanimously granted that the error had been mine and nobody's else at all, an odd prosaic pleasantness set itself straight up, substitutionally, over the whole ground, which it swept clear of every single premeditated effect. It made one's perceptive condition purely profane, reduced it somehow to having rather the excess of awkwardness than the excess of felicity to reckon with; yet still again, as I say, enabled a compromise to work.

The compromise in fact worked beautifully under my renewal of impression—for which a second visit at Eaton Place offered occasion; and this even though I had to interweave with the scene as best I might a highly complicating influence. To speak of James Russell Lowell's influence as above all complicating on any scene to the interest of which he contributed may superficially seem a perverse appreciation of it; and yet in the light of that truth only do I recover the full sense of his value, his interest, the moving moral of his London adventure—to find myself already bumping so straight against which gives me, I confess, a sufficiently portentous shake. He comes in, as it were, by a force not to be denied, as soon as I look at him again—as soon as I find him for instance on the doorstep in Eaton Place at the hour of my too approaching it for luncheon as he had just done. There he is, with the whole question of him, at once before me, and literally superimposed by that fact on any minor essence. I quake, positively, with the apprehension of the commemorative dance he may lead me; but for the moment, just here, I steady myself with an effort and go in with him to his having the Laureate's personal acquaintance, by every symptom, and rather to my surprise, all to make. Mrs. Tennyson's luncheon table was an open feast, with places for possible when not assured guests; and no one but the American Minister, scarce

ore than just installed, and his extremely attached compatriot sat down
first with our gracious hostess. The board considerably stretched, and
fter it had been indicated to Lowell that he had best sit at the end near
he window, where the Bard would presently join him, I remained, near
ur hostess, separated from him for some little time by an unpeopled waste.
Hallam came in all genially and auspiciously, yet only to brush us with his
blessing and say he was lunching elsewhere, and my wonder meanwhile hung
about the representative of my country, who, though partaking of offered
ood, appeared doomed to disconnection from us. I may say at once that
my wonder was always unable *not* to hang about this admired and cherished
friend when other persons, especially of the eminent order, were concerned
n the scene. The case was quite other for the unshared relation, or when it
was shared by one or other of three or four of our common friends who had
he gift of determining happily the pitch of ease; suspense, not to say anxiety,
s to the possible turn or drift of the affair quite dropped—I rested then, we
like rested, I ever felt, in a golden confidence. This last was so definitely not
he note of my attention to him, so far as I might indulge it, in the wider
ocial world, that I shall not scruple, occasion offering, to inquire into the
easons of the difference. For I can only see the ghosts of my friends, by this
oken, as "my" J. R. L. and whoever; which means that my imagination, of
he wanton life of which these remarks pretend but to form the record, had
ppropriated them, under the prime contact—from the moment the prime
ontact had successfully worked—once for all, and contributed the light in
which they were constantly exposed.

Yes, delightful I shall undertake finding it, and perhaps even making
t, to read J. R. L.'s exposure back into *its* light; which I in fact see begin
o shine for me more amply during those very minutes of our wait for our
distinguished host and even the several that followed the latter's arrival and
his seating himself opposite the unknown guest, whose identity he had failed
o grasp. Nothing, exactly, could have made dear Lowell more "my" Lowell, as
have presumed to figure him, than the stretch of uncertainty so supervening
nd which, in its form of silence at first completely unbroken between the
wo poets, rapidly took on for me monstrous proportions. I conversed with
my gentle neighbour during what seemed an eternity—really but hearing, as

the minutes sped, all that Tennyson didn't say to Lowell and all that Lowell wouldn't on any such compulsion as that say to Tennyson. I like, however, to hang again upon the hush—for the sweetness of the relief of its break by the fine Tennysonian growl. I had never dreamed, no, of a growling Tennyson— had too utterly otherwise fantasticated; but no line of Locksley Hall rolled out as I was to happen soon after to hear it, could have been sweeter than the interrogative sound of "Do you know anything about *Lowell*?" launched on the chance across the table and crowned at once by Mrs. Tennyson's anxious quaver: "Why, my dear, this *is* Mr. Lowell!" The clearance took place successfully enough, and the incident, I am quite aware, seems to shrink with it; in spite of which I still cherish the reduced reminiscence for its connections: so far as my vision of Lowell was concerned they began at that moment so to multiply. A belated guest or two more came in, and I wish could for my modesty's sake refer to this circumstance alone the fact that nothing more of the occasion survives for me save the intense but restricted glow of certain instants, in another room, to which we had adjourned for smoking and where my alarmed sense of the Bard's restriction to giving what he had as a bard only became under a single turn of his hand a vision of quite general munificence. Incredibly, inconceivably, he had *read*—and not only read but admired, and not only admired but understandingly referred referred, time and some accident aiding, the appreciated object, a short tale I had lately put forth, to its actually present author, who could scarce believe his ears on hearing the thing superlatively commended; pronounced, that is, by the illustrious speaker, more to his taste than no matter what other like attempt. Nothing would induce me to disclose the title of the piece, which has little to do with the matter; my point is but in its having on the spot been matter of pure romance to me that I was there and positively so addressed. For it was a solution, the happiest in the world, and from which I at once extracted enormities of pleasure: my relation to whatever had bewildered me simply became perfect: the author of In Memoriam had "liked" my own twenty pages, and his doing so was a gage of his grace in which I felt I should rest forever—in which I have in fact rested to this hour. My own basis of liking—such a blessed supersession of all worryings and wonderings!—was accordingly established, and has met every demand made of it.

Greatest was to have been, I dare say, the demand to which I felt it exposed by the drive over to Aldworth with Mrs. Greville which I noted above and which took place, if I am not mistaken, on the morrow of our drive to Witley. A different shade of confidence and comfort, I make out, accompanied this experiment: I believed more, for reasons I shall not now attempt to recover, in the furthermost maintenance of our flying bridge, the final piers of which, it was indubitable, *had* at Witley given way. What could have been moreover less like G. H. Lewes's valedictory hurl back upon us of the printed appeal in which I was primarily concerned than that so recent and so directly opposed passage of the Eaton Place smoking-room, thanks to which I could nurse a certified security all along the road? I surrendered to security, I perhaps even grossly took my ease in it; and I was to breathe from beginning to end of our visit, which began with our sitting again at luncheon, an air—so unlike that of Witley!—in which it seemed to me frankly that nothing but the blest obvious, or at least the blest outright, could so much as attempt to live. These elements hung sociably and all auspiciously about us—it was a large and simple and almost empty occasion; yet empty without embarrassment, rather as from a certain high guardedness or defensiveness of situation, literally indeed from the material, the local sublimity, the fact of our all upliftedly hanging together over one of the grandest sweeps of view in England. Remembered passages again people, however, in their proportion, the excess of opportunity; each with that conclusive note of the outright all unadorned. What could have partaken more of this quality for instance than the question I was startled to hear launched before we had left the table by the chance of Mrs. Greville's having happened to mention in some connection one of her French relatives, Mademoiselle Laure de Sade? It had fallen on my own ear—the mention at least had—with a certain effect of unconscious provocation; but this was as nothing to its effect on the ear of our host. "De Sade?" he at once exclaimed with interest—and with the consequence, I may frankly add, of my wondering almost to ecstasy, that is to the ecstasy of curiosity, to what length he would proceed. He proceeded admirably—admirably for the triumph of simplification—to the very greatest length imaginable, as was signally promoted by the fact that clearly no one present, with a single exception, recognised the name or the nature of the scandalous, the long ignored, the at last all but unnameable author; least of all the gentle relative of Mademoiselle Laure, who listened with the blankest grace to her friend's enumeration of his titles to infamy, among which that of his most notorious work was pronounced. It was the homeliest, frankest, most domestic passage, as who should say, and most remarkable for leaving none of us save myself, by my impression, in the least embarrassed or bewildered; largely, I think, because of the failure—a failure the most charmingly flat— of all measure on the part of auditors and speaker alike of what might be intended or understood, of what, in fine, the latter was talking about.

He struck me in truth as neither knowing nor communicating knowledge, and I recall how I felt this note in his own case to belong to that general intimation with which the whole air was charged of the want of proportion between the great spaces and reaches and echoes commanded, the great eminence attained, and the quantity and variety of experience supposable. So to discriminate was in a manner to put one's hand on the key, and thereby to find one's self in presence of a rare and anomalous, but still scarcely the less beautiful fact. The assured and achieved conditions, the serenity, the security, the success, to put it vulgarly, shone in the light of their easiest law—that by which they emerge early from the complication of life, the great adventure of sensibility, and find themselves determined once for all, fortunately fixed, all consecrated and consecrating. If I should speak of this impression as that of glory without history, that of the poetic character more worn than paid for, or at least more saved than spent, I should doubtless much over-emphasise; but such, or something like it, was none the less the explanation that met one's own fond fancy of the scene after one had cast about for it. For I allow myself thus to repeat that I was so moved to cast about, and perhaps at no moment more than during the friendly analysis of the reputation of M. de Sade. Was I not present at some undreamed- of demonstration of the absence of the remoter real, the real other than immediate and exquisite, other than guaranteed and enclosed, in landscape, friendship, fame, above all in consciousness of awaited and admired and self- consistent inspiration?

The question was indeed to be effectively answered for me, and everything meanwhile continued to play into this prevision—even to the pleasant growling note heard behind me, as the Bard followed with Mrs. Greville, who had permitted herself apparently some mild extravagance of homage: "Oh yes, you may do what you like—so long as you don't kiss me before the cabman!" The allusion was explained for us, if I remember—a matter of some more or less recent leave-taking of admirer and admired in London on his putting her down at her door after being taken to the play or wherever; between the rugged humour of which reference and the other just commemorated there wasn't a pin to choose, it struck me, for a certain old-time Lincolnshire ease or comfortable stay-at-home license. But it was later on, when, my introductress having accompanied us, I sat upstairs with him in his study, that he might read to us some poem of his own that we should venture to propose, it was then that mystifications dropped, that everything in the least dislocated fell into its place, and that image and picture stamped themselves strongly and finally, or to the point even, as I recover it, of leaving me almost too little to wonder about. He had not got a third of the way through Locksley Hall, which, my choice given me, I had made bold to suggest he should spout—for I had already heard him spout in Eaton Place—before I had begun to wonder that I didn't wonder, didn't at least wonder more consumedly; as a very little while back I should have made sure of my doing on any such prodigious occasion. I sat at one of the windows that hung over space, noting how the windy, watery autumn day, sometimes sheeting it all with rain, called up the dreary, dreary moorland or the long dun wolds; I pinched myself for the determination of my identity and hung on the reader's deep-voiced chant for the credibility of his: I asked myself in fine why, in complete deviation from everything that would have seemed from far back certain for the case, I failed to swoon away under the heaviest pressure I had doubtless ever known the romantic situation bring to bear. So lucidly all the while I considered, so detachedly I judged, so dissentingly, to tell the whole truth, I listened; pinching myself, as I say, not at all to keep from swooning, but much rather to set up some rush of sensibility. It was all interesting, it was at least all odd; but why in the name of poetic justice had one anciently heaved and flushed with one's own recital of the splendid stuff if one was now only to sigh in secret "Oh dear, oh dear"? The author lowered the whole pitch, that of expression, that of interpretation above all; I heard him, in cool surprise, take even more out of his verse than he had put in, and so bring me back to the point I had immediately and privately made, the point that he wasn't Tennysonian. I felt him as he went on and on lose that character beyond repair, and no effect of the organ-roll, of monotonous majesty, no suggestion of the long echo, availed at all to save it. What the case came to for me, I take it—and by the case I mean the intellectual, the artistic— was that it lacked the intelligence, the play of discrimination, I should have taken for granted in it, and thereby, brooding monster that I was, born to discriminate *à tout propos*, lacked the interest.

Detached I have mentioned that I had become, and it was doubtless at such a rate high time for that; though I hasten to repeat that with the close of the incident I was happily able to feel a new sense in the whole connection established. My critical reaction hadn't in the least invalidated our great man's being a Bard—it had in fact made him and left him more a Bard than ever: it had only settled to my perception as not before what a Bard might and mightn't be. The character was just a rigid idiosyncrasy, to which everything in the man conformed, but which supplied nothing outside of itself, and which above all was not intellectually wasteful or heterogeneous, conscious as it could only be of its intrinsic breadth and weight. On two or three occasions of the aftertime I was to hear Browning read out certain of his finest pages, and this exactly with all the exhibition of point and authority, the expressive particularisation, so to speak, that I had missed on the part of the Laureate; an observation through which the author of Men and Women appeared, in spite of the beauty and force of his demonstration, as little as possible a Bard. He particularised if ever a man did, was heterogeneous and profane, composed of pieces and patches that betrayed some creak of joints, and addicted to the excursions from which these were brought home; so that he had to *prove* himself a poet, almost against all presumptions, and with all the assurance and all the character he could use. Was not this last in especial, the character, so close to the surface, with which Browning fairly bristled, what was most to come out in his personal delivery of the fruit of his genius? It came out almost to harshness; but the result was that what e read showed extraordinary life. During that audition at Aldworth the uestion seemed on the contrary not of life at all—save, that is, of one's own; hich was exactly not the question. With all the resonance of the chant, the hole thing was yet *still*, with all the long swing of its motion it yet remained here it was—heaving doubtless grandly enough up and down and beautiful watch as through the superposed veils of its long self-consciousness. By l of which I don't mean to say that I was not, on the day at Aldworth, noroughly reconciled to learning what a Bard consisted of; for that came as on as I had swallowed my own mistake—the mistake of having supposed ennyson something subtly other than one. I had supposed, probably, such n impossibility, had, to repeat my term, so absurdly fantasticated, that the ng journey round and about the truth no more than served me right; just as fter all it at last left me quite content.

VII

It left me moreover, I become aware—or at least it now leaves me—fingering the loose ends of this particular free stretch of my tapestry; so that with my perhaps even extravagant aversion to loose ends, I can but try for a moment to interweave them. There dangles again for me least confusedly, think, the vision of a dinner at Mrs. Greville's—and I like even to remember that Cadogan Place, where memories hang thick for me, was the scene of it—which took its light from the presence of Louisa Lady Waterford, who took hers in turn from that combination of rare beauty with rare talent which the previous Victorian age had for many years not ceased to acclaim. It insist on coming back to me with the utmost vividness that Lady Waterford was illustrational, historically, preciously so, meeting one's largest demand for the blest recovery, when possible, of some glimmer of the sense of personal beauty to say nothing of personal "accomplishment," as our fathers were appointed to enjoy it. Scarce to be sated that form of wonder, to my own imagination I confess—so that I fairly believe there was no moment at which I wouldn't have been ready to turn my back for the time even on the most triumphant actuality of form and feature if a chance apprehension of a like force as it played on the sensibility of the past had competed. And this for a reason I fear I can scarce explain—unless, when I come to consider it, by the perversity of a conviction that the conditions of beauty have improved, though those of character, in the fine old sense, may not, and that with these the measure of it is more just, the appreciation, as who should say, more competent and the effect more completely attained.

What the question seems thus to come to would be a consuming curiosity as to any cited old case of the spell in the very interest of one's catching it comparatively "out"; in the interest positively of the likelihood of one's doing so, and this in the face of so many great testifying portraits. My private perversity, as I here glance at it, has had its difficulties—most of all possibly that of one's addiction, in growing older, to allowing a supreme force to one's earlier, even one's earliest, estimates of physical felicity; or in other words that of the felt impulse to leave the palm for good looks to those who have reached out to it through the medium of our own history. If the conditions *grow* better for them why then should we have almost the habit of thinking better of our handsome folk dead than of our living?—and even to the very point of not resenting on the part of others similarly affected the wail of wonder as to what has strangely "become" of the happy types *d'antan*. I dodge that inquiry just now—we may meet it again; noting simply the fact that "old" pretenders to the particular crown I speak of—and in the sense especially of the pretension made rather for than by them—offered to my eyes a greater interest than the new, whom I was ready enough to take for granted, as one for the most part easily could; belonging as it exactly did on the other hand to the interest of their elders that *this* couldn't be so taken. That was just the attraction of the latter claim—that the grounds of it had to be made out, puzzled out verily on occasion, but that when they were recognised they had a force all their own. One would have liked to be able to clear the distinction between the new and the old of all ambiguity—explain, that is, how little the superficially invidious term was sometimes noted as having in common with the elderly: so much was it a clear light held up to the question that truly beautiful persons might be old without being elderly. Their juniors couldn't be new, unfortunately, without being youthful—unfortunately because the fact of youth, so far from dispelling ambiguity, positively introduced it. One made up one's mind thus that the only sure specimens were, and had to be, those acquainted with time, and with whom time, on its side, was acquainted; those in fine who had borne the test and still looked at it face to face. These were of one's own period of course—one looked at *them* face to, face; one blessedly hadn't to consider them by hearsay or to refer to any portrait of them for proof: indeed in presence of the resisting, the gained, cases one found one's self practically averse to old facts or old traditions of portraiture, accompanied by no matter what names.

All of which leads by an avenue I trust not unduly majestic up to that hour of contemplation during which I could see quite enough for the major interest what was meant by Lady Waterford's great reputation. Nothing could in fact have been more informing than so to see what was meant, than so copiously to share with admirers who had had their vision and passed on;

for if I spoke above of her image as illustrational this is because it affected me on the spot as so diffusing information. My impression was of course but the old story—to which my reader will feel himself treated, I fear, to satiety: when once I had drawn the curtain for the light shed by this or that or the other personal presence upon the society more or less intimately concerned in producing it the last thing I could think of was to darken the scene again. For this right or this wrong reason then Mrs. Greville's admirable guest struck me as flooding it; indebted in the highest degree to every art by which a commended appearance may have formed the habit of still suggesting commendation, she certainly—to my imagination at least—triumphed over time in the sense that if the years, in their generosity, went on helping her to live, her grace returned the favour by paying life back to them. I mean that she reanimated for the fond analyst the age in which persons of her type could so greatly flourish—it being ever so pertinently of her type, or at least of that of the age, that she was regarded as having cast the spell of genius as well as of beauty. She painted, and on the largest scale, with all confidence and facility, and nothing could have contributed more, by my sense, to what I glance at again as her illustrational value than the apparently widespread appreciation of this fact—taken together, that is, with one's own impression of the work of her hand. There it was that, like Mrs. Greville herself, yet in a still higher degree, she bore witness to the fine old felicity of the fortunate and the "great" under the "old" order which would have made it so good then to live could one but have been in their shoes. She determined in me, I remember, a renewed perception of the old order, a renewed insistence on one's having come just in time to see it begin to stretch back: a little earlier one wouldn't have had the light for this perhaps, and a little later it would have receded too much.

The precious persons, the surviving figures, who held up, as I may call it, the light were still here and there to be met; my sense being that the last of them, at least for any vision of mine, has now quite gone and that illustration—not to let that term slip—accordingly fails. We all now illustrate together, in higgledy-piggledy fashion, or as a vast monotonous mob, our own wonderful period and order, and nothing else; whereby the historic imagination, under its acuter need of facing backward, gropes before it with a vain gesture, missing, or all but missing, the concrete *other*, always other, specimen which has volumes to give where hearsay has only snippets. The old, as we call it, I recognise, doesn't disappear all at once; the *ancien régime* of our commonest reference survived the Revolution of our most horrific in patches and scraps, and I bring myself to say that even at my present writing I am aware of more than one individual on the scene about me touched *comparatively* with the elder grace. (I think of the difference between these persons and so nearly all other persons as a grace for reasons that become perfectly clear in the immediate presence of the former, but of which a generalising account is difficult.) None the less it used to be one of the finest of pleasures to acclaim and cherish, in case of meeting them, one and another of the *complete* examples of the conditions irrecoverable, even if, as I have already noted, they were themselves least intelligently conscious of these; and for the enjoyment of that critical emotion to draw one's own wanton line between the past and the present. The happy effect of such apparitions as Lady Waterford, to whom I thus undisseverably cling, though I might give her after all much like company, was that they made one draw it just where they might most profit from it. They profited in that they recruited my group of the fatuously fortunate, the class, as I seemed to see it, that had had the longest and happiest innings in history—happier and longer, on the whole, even than their congeners of the old French time—and for whom the future wasn't going to be, by most signs, anything like as bland and benedictory as the past. They placed *themselves* in the right perspective for appreciation, and did it quite without knowing, which was half the interest; did it simply by showing themselves with all the right grace and the right assurance. It was as if they had come up to the very edge of the ground that was going to begin to fail them; yet looking over it, looking on and on always, with a confidence still unalarmed. One would have turned away certainly from the sight of any actual catastrophe, wouldn't have watched the ground nearly fail, in a particular case, without a sense of gross indelicacy. I can scarcely say how vivid I felt the drama so preparing might become—that of the lapse of immemorial protection, that of the finally complete exposure of the immemorially protected. It might take place rather more intensely before the footlights of one's inner vision than on the trodden stage of Cadogan Place or wherever, but it corresponded none the less to realities all the while in course of enactment and which only wanted the attentive enough spectator. Nothing should I evermore see comparable to the large fond consensus of admiration enjoyed by my beatific fellow-guest's imputed command of the very palette of the Venetian and other masters—Titian's, Bonifazio's, Rubens's, where did the delightful agreement on the subject stop? and never again should a noble lady be lifted so still further aloft on the ecstatic breath of connoisseurship.

This last consciousness, confirming my impression of a climax that could only decline, didn't break upon me all at once but spread itself through a couple of subsequent occasions into which my remembrance of the dinner at Mrs. Greville's was richly to play. The first of these was a visit to an exhibition of Lady Waterford's paintings held, in Carlton House Terrace, under the roof of a friend of the artist, and, as it enriched the hour also to be able to feel, a friend, one of the most generously gracious, of my own; during which the reflection that "they" had indeed had their innings, and were still splendidly using for the purpose the very fag-end of the waning time, mixed itself for me with all the "wonderful colour" framed and arrayed, that blazed from the walls of the kindly great room, lent for the advantage of a charity, and lost itself in the general chorus of immense comparison and tender consecration. Later on a few days spent at a house of the greatest beauty and interest in Northumberland did wonders to round off my view; the place, occupied for the time by genial tenants, belonged to the family of Lady Waterford's husband and fairly bristled, it might be said, with coloured designs from her brush....

THE PATAGONIA

I

THE houses were dark in the August night and the perspective of Beacon Street, with its double chain of lamps, was a foreshortened desert. The club on the hill alone, from its semi-cylindrical front, projected a glow upon the dusky vagueness of the Common, and as I passed it I heard in the hot stillness the click of a pair of billiard-balls. As "every one" was out of town perhaps the servants, in the extravagance of their leisure, were profaning the tables. The heat was insufferable and I thought with joy of the morrow, of the deck of the steamer, the freshening breeze, the sense of getting out to sea. I was even glad of what I had learned in the afternoon at the office of the company—that at the eleventh hour an old ship with a lower standard of speed had been put on in place of the vessel in which I had taken my passage. America was roasting, England might very well be stuffy, and a slow passage (which at that season of the year would probably also be a fine one) was a guarantee of ten or twelve days of fresh air.

I strolled down the hill without meeting a creature, though I could see through the palings of the Common that that recreative expanse was peopled with dim forms. I remembered Mrs. Nettlepoint's house—she lived in those days (they are not so distant, but there have been changes) on the water-side, a little way beyond the spot at which the Public Garden terminates; and I reflected that like myself she would be spending the night in Boston if it were true that, as had been mentioned to me a few days before at Mount Desert, she was to embark on the morrow for Liverpool. I presently saw this appearance confirmed by a light above her door and in two or three of her windows, and I determined to ask for her, having nothing to do till bedtime. I had come out simply to pass an hour, leaving my hotel to the blaze of its gas and the perspiration of its porters; but it occurred to me that my old friend might very *well* not know of the substitution of the *Patagonia* for the *Scandinavia*, so that I should be doing her a service to prepare her mind. Besides, I could offer to help her, to look after her in the morning: lone women are grateful for support in taking ship for far countries.

It came to me indeed as I stood on her door-step that as she had a son she might not after all be so lone; yet I remembered at the same time that Jasper Nettlepoint was not quite a young man to lean upon, having—as I at least supposed—a life of his own and tastes and habits which had long since diverted him from the maternal side. If he did happen just now to be at home my solicitude would of course seem officious; for in his many wanderings—I believed he had roamed all over the globe—he would certainly have learned how to manage. None the less, in fine, I was very glad to show Mrs. Nettlepoint I thought of her. With my long absence I had lost sight of her; but I had liked her of old, she had been a good friend to my sisters, and I had in regard to her that sense which is pleasant to those who in general have gone astray or got detached, the sense that she at least knew all about me. I could trust her at any time to tell people I was respectable. Perhaps I was conscious of how little I deserved this indulgence when it came over me that I hadn't been near her for ages. The measure of that neglect was given by my vagueness of mind about Jasper. However, I really belonged nowadays to a different generation; I was more the mother's contemporary than the son's.

Mrs. Nettlepoint was at home: I found her in her back drawing-room, where the wide windows opened to the water. The room was dusky—it was too hot for lamps—and she sat slowly moving her fan and looking out on the little arm of the sea which is so pretty at night, reflecting the lights of Cambridgeport and Charlestown. I supposed she was musing on the loved ones she was to leave behind, her married daughters, her grandchildren; but she struck a note more specifically Bostonian as she said to me, pointing with her fan to the Back Bay: "I shall see nothing more charming than that over there, you know!" She made me very welcome, but her son had told her about the *Patagonia*, for which she was sorry, as this would mean a longer voyage. She was a poor creature in any boat and mainly confined to her cabin even in weather extravagantly termed fine—as if any weather could be fine at sea.

"Ah then your son's going with you?" I asked.

"Here he comes, he'll tell you for himself much better than I can pretend to." Jasper Nettlepoint at that moment joined us, dressed in white flannel nd carrying a large fan. "Well, my dear, have you decided?" his mother ontinued with no scant irony. "He hasn't yet made up his mind, and we sail t ten o'clock!"

"What does it matter when my things are put up?" the young man said. There's no crowd at this moment; there will be cabins to spare. I'm waiting r a telegram—that will settle it. I just walked up to the club to see if it was ome—they'll send it there because they suppose this house unoccupied. Not et, but I shall go back in twenty minutes."

"Mercy, how you rush about in this temperature!" the poor lady xclaimed while I reflected that it was perhaps *his* billiard-balls I had heard en minutes before. I was sure he was fond of billiards.

"Rush? not in the least. I take it uncommon easy."

"Ah I'm bound to say you do!" Mrs. Nettlepoint returned with nconsequence. I guessed at a certain tension between the pair and a want f consideration on the young man's part, arising perhaps from selfishness. His mother was nervous, in suspense, wanting to be at rest as to whether she hould have his company on the voyage or be obliged to struggle alone. But s he stood there smiling and slowly moving his fan he struck me somehow s a person on whom this fact wouldn't sit too heavily. He was of the type of hose whom other people worry about, not of those who worry about other eople. Tall and strong, he had a handsome face, with a round head and lose-curling hair; the whites of his eyes and the enamel of his teeth, under his rown moustache, gleamed vaguely in the lights of the Back Bay. I made out hat he was sunburnt, as if he lived much in the open air, and that he looked ntelligent but also slightly brutal, though not in a morose way. His brutality, f he had any, was bright and finished. I had to tell him who I was, but even hen I saw how little he placed me and that my explanations gave me in his nind no great identity or at any rate no great importance. I foresaw that he vould in intercourse make me feel sometimes very young and sometimes ery old, caring himself but little which. He mentioned, as if to show our ompanion that he might safely be left to his own devices, that he had once tarted from London to Bombay at three quarters of an hour's notice.

75

"Yes, and it must have been pleasant for the people you were with!"

"Oh the people I was with—!" he returned; and his tone appeared to signify that such people would always have to come off as they could. He asked if there were no cold drinks in the house, no lemonade, no iced syrups; in such weather something of that sort ought always to be kept going. When his mother remarked that surely at the club they *were* kept going he went on: "Oh yes, I had various things there; but you know I've walked down the hill since. One should have something at either end. May I ring and see?" He rang while Mrs. Nettlepoint observed that with the people they had in the house, an establishment reduced naturally at such a moment to its simplest expression—they were burning up candle-ends and there were no luxuries— she wouldn't answer for the service. The matter ended in her leaving the room in quest of cordials with the female domestic who had arrived in response to the bell and in whom Jasper's appeal aroused no visible intelligence.

She remained away some time and I talked with her son, who was sociable but desultory and kept moving over the place, always with his fan, as if he were properly impatient. Sometimes he seated himself an instant on the window-sill, and then I made him out in fact thoroughly good-looking—a fine brown clean young athlete. He failed to tell me on what special contingency his decision depended; he only alluded familiarly to an expected telegram, and I saw he was probably fond at no time of the trouble of explanations. His mother's absence was a sign that when it might be a question of gratifying him she had grown used to spare no pains, and I fancied her rummaging in some close storeroom, among old preserve-pots, while the dull maid-servant held the candle awry. I don't know whether this same vision was in his own eyes; at all events it didn't prevent his saying suddenly, as he looked at his watch, that I must excuse him—he should have to go back to the club. He would return in half an hour—or in less. He walked away and I sat there alone, conscious, on the dark dismantled simplified scene, in the deep silence that rests on American towns during the hot season—there was now and then a far cry or a plash in the water, and at intervals the tinkle of the bells of the horse-cars on the long bridge, slow in the suffocating night—of the strange influence, half-sweet, half-sad, that abides in houses uninhabited or about to become so, in places muffled and bereaved, where the unheeded sofas and patient belittered tables seem (like the disconcerted dogs, to whom everything is alike sinister) to recognise the eve of a journey.

After a while I heard the sound of voices, of steps, the rustle of dresses, and I looked round, supposing these things to denote the return of Mrs. Nettlepoint and her handmaiden with the refection prepared for her son. What I saw however was two other female forms, visitors apparently just admitted, and now ushered into the room. They were not announced—the servant turned her back on them and rambled off to our hostess. They advanced in a wavering tentative unintroduced way—partly, I could see, because the place was dark and partly because their visit was in its nature experimental, a flight of imagination or a stretch of confidence. One of the ladies was stout and the other slim, and I made sure in a moment that one was talkative and the other reserved. It was further to be discerned that one was elderly and the other young, as well as that the fact of their unlikeness didn't prevent their being mother and daughter. Mrs. Nettlepoint reappeared in a very few minutes, but the interval had sufficed to establish a communication—really copious for the occasion—between the strangers and the unknown gentleman whom they found in possession, hat and stick in hand. This was not my doing—for what had I to go upon?—and still less was it the doing of the younger and the more indifferent, or less courageous, lady. She spoke but once—when her companion informed me that she was going out to Europe the next day to be married. Then she protested "Oh mother!" in a tone that struck me in the darkness as doubly odd, exciting my curiosity to see her face.

It had taken the elder woman but a moment to come to that, and to various other things, after I had explained that I myself was waiting for Mrs. Nettlepoint, who would doubtless soon come back.

"Well, she won't know me—I guess she hasn't ever heard much about me," the good lady said; "but I've come from Mrs. Allen and I guess that will make it all right. I presume you know Mrs. Allen?"

I was unacquainted with this influential personage, but I assented vaguely to the proposition. Mrs. Allen's emissary was good-humoured and familiar, but rather appealing than insistent (she remarked that if her friend *had* found time to come in the afternoon—she had so much to do, being just up for the day, that she couldn't be sure—it would be all right); and somehow even before she mentioned Merrimac Avenue (they had come all the way from there) my imagination had associated her with that indefinite social limbo known to the properly-constituted Boston mind as the South End—a nebulous region which condenses here and there into a pretty face, in which the daughters are an "improvement" on the mothers and are sometimes acquainted with gentlemen more gloriously domiciled, gentlemen whose wives and sisters are in turn not acquainted with them.

When at last Mrs. Nettlepoint came in, accompanied by candles and by a tray laden with glasses of coloured fluid which emitted a cool tinkling, I was in a position to officiate as master of the ceremonies, to introduce Mrs. Mavis and Miss Grace Mavis, to represent that Mrs. Allen had recommended them—nay, had urged them—just to come that way, informally and without fear; Mrs. Allen who had been prevented only by the pressure of occupations so characteristic of her (especially when up from Mattapoisett for a few hours' desperate shopping) from herself calling in the course of the day to explain who they were and what was the favour they had to ask of her benevolent friend. Good-natured women understand each other even when so divided as to sit residentially above and below the salt, as who should say; by which token our hostess had quickly mastered the main facts: Mrs. Allen's visit that morning in Merrimac Avenue to talk of Mrs. Amber's great idea, the classes at the public schools in vacation (she was interested with an equal charity to that of Mrs. Mavis—even in such weather!—in those of the South End) for games and exercises and music, to keep the poor unoccupied children out of the streets; then the revelation that it had suddenly been settled almost from one hour to the other that Grace should sail for Liverpool, Mr. Porterfield at last being ready. He was taking a little holiday; his mother was with him, they had come over from Paris to see some of the celebrated old buildings in England, and he had telegraphed to say that if Grace would start right off they would just finish it up and be married. It often happened that when things had dragged on that way for years they were all huddled up at the end. Of course in such a case she, Mrs. Mavis, had had to fly round. Her daughter's passage was taken, but it seemed too dreadful she should make her journey all alone, the first time she had ever been at sea, without any companion or escort. *She* couldn't go—Mr. Mavis was too sick: she hadn't even been able to get him off to the seaside.

"Well, Mrs. Nettlepoint's going in that ship," Mrs. Allen had said; and she had represented that nothing was simpler than to give her the girl in charge. When Mrs. Mavis had replied that this was all very well but that she didn't know the lady, Mrs. Allen had declared that that didn't make a speck of difference, for Mrs. Nettlepoint was kind enough for anything. It was easy enough to *know* her, if that was all the trouble! All Mrs. Mavis would have to do would be to go right up to her next morning, when she took her daughter to the ship (she would see her there on the deck with her party) and tell her fair and square what she wanted. Mrs. Nettlepoint had daughters herself and would easily understand. Very likely she'd even look after Grace a little on the other side, in such a queer situation, going out alone to the gentleman she was engaged to: she'd just help her, like a good Samaritan, to turn round before she was married. Mr. Porterfield seemed to think they wouldn't wait long, once she was there: they would have it right over at the American consul's. Mrs. Allen had said it would perhaps be better still to go and see Mrs. Nettlepoint beforehand, that day, to tell her what they wanted: then they wouldn't seem to spring it on her just as she was leaving. She herself (Mrs. Allen) would call and say a word for them if she could save ten minutes before catching her train. If she hadn't come it was because she hadn't saved her ten minutes but she had made them feel that they must come all the same. Mrs. Mavis liked that better, because on the ship in the morning there would be such a confusion. She didn't think her daughter would be any trouble— conscientiously she didn't. It was just to have some one to speak to her and not sally forth like a servant-girl going to a situation.

"I see, I'm to act as a sort of bridesmaid and to give her away," Mrs. Nettlepoint obligingly said. Kind enough in fact for anything, she showed on this occasion that it was easy enough to know her. There is notoriously nothing less desirable than an imposed aggravation of effort at sea, but she accepted without betrayed dismay the burden of the young lady's dependence and allowed her, as Mrs. Mavis said, to hook herself on. She evidently had the habit of patience, and her reception of her visitors' story reminded me afresh—I was reminded of it whenever I returned to my native land—that my dear compatriots are the people in the world who most freely take mutual accommodation for granted. They have always had to help themselves, and have rather magnanimously failed to learn just where helping others is distinguishable from that. In no country are there fewer forms and more reciprocities.

It was doubtless not singular that the ladies from Merrimac Avenue shouldn't feel they were importunate: what was striking was that Mrs. Nettlepoint didn't appear to suspect it. However, she would in any case have thought it inhuman to show this—though I could see that under the surface she was amused at everything the more expressive of the pilgrims from the South End took for granted. I scarce know whether the attitude of the younger visitor added or not to the merit of her good nature. Mr. Porterfield's intended took no part in the demonstration, scarcely spoke, sat looking at the Back Bay and the lights on the long bridge. She declined the lemonade and the other mixtures which, at Mrs. Nettlepoint's request, I offered her, while her mother partook freely of everything and I reflected—for I as freely drained a glass or two in which the ice tinkled—that Mr. Jasper had better hurry back if he wished to enjoy these luxuries.

Was the effect of the young woman's reserve meanwhile ungracious, or was it only natural that in her particular situation she shouldn't have a flow of compliment at her command? I noticed that Mrs. Nettlepoint looked at her often, and certainly though she was undemonstrative Miss Mavis was interesting. The candlelight enabled me to see that though not in the very first flower of her youth she was still fresh and handsome. Her eyes and hair were dark, her face was pale, and she held up her head as if, with its thick braids and everything else involved in it, it were an appurtenance she wasn't ashamed of. If her mother was excellent and common she was not common—not at least flagrantly so—and perhaps also not excellent. At all events she wouldn't be, in appearance at least, a dreary appendage; which in the case of a person "hooking on" was always something gained. Was because something of a romantic or pathetic interest usually attaches to good creature who has been the victim of a "long engagement" that this oung lady made an impression on me from the first—favoured as I had een so quickly with this glimpse of her history? I could charge her certainly ith no positive appeal; she only held her tongue and smiled, and her smile orrected whatever suggestion might have forced itself upon me that the spirit ithin her was dead—the spirit of that promise of which she found herself oomed to carry out the letter.

What corrected it less, I must add, was an odd recollection which athered vividness as I listened to it—a mental association evoked by the ame of Mr. Porterfield. Surely I had a personal impression, over-smeared nd confused, of the gentleman who was waiting at Liverpool, or who resently would be, for Mrs. Nettlepoint's protégée. I had met him, known im, some time, somewhere, somehow, on the other side. Wasn't he studying omething, very hard, somewhere—probably in Paris—ten years before, and idn't he make extraordinarily neat drawings, linear and architectural? Didn't e go to a table d'hôte, at two francs twenty-five, in the Rue Bonaparte, hich I then frequented, and didn't he wear spectacles and a Scotch plaid rranged in a manner which seemed to say "I've trustworthy information that at's the way they do it in the Highlands"? Wasn't he exemplary to positive ritation, and very poor, poor to positive oppression, so that I supposed he ad no overcoat and his tartan would be what he slept under at night? Wasn't e working very hard still, and wouldn't he be, in the natural course, not yet atisfied that he had found his feet or knew enough to launch out? He would e a man of long preparations—Miss Mavis's white face seemed to speak to ne of that. It struck me that if I had been in love with her I shouldn't have eeded to lay such a train for the closer approach. Architecture was his line nd he was a pupil of the École des Beaux Arts. This reminiscence grew so uch more vivid with me that at the end of ten minutes I had an odd sense f knowing—by implication—a good deal about the young lady.

Even after it was settled that Mrs. Nettlepoint would do everything ossible for her the other visitor sat sipping our iced liquid and telling how low" Mr. Mavis had been. At this period the girl's silence struck me as still more conscious, partly perhaps because she deprecated her mother's free flow—she was enough of an "improvement" to measure that—and partly because she was too distressed by the idea of leaving her infirm, her perhaps dying father. It wasn't indistinguishable that they were poor and that she would take out a very small purse for her trousseau. For Mr. Porterfield to make up the sum his own case would have had moreover greatly to change. If he had enriched himself by the successful practice of his profession I had encountered no edifice he had reared—his reputation hadn't come to my ears.

Mrs. Nettlepoint notified her new friends that she was a very inactive person at sea: she was prepared to suffer to the full with Miss Mavis, but not prepared to pace the deck with her, to struggle with her, to accompany her to meals. To this the girl replied that she would trouble her little, she was sure she was convinced she should prove a wretched sailor and spend the voyage on her back. Her mother scoffed at this picture, prophesying perfect weather and a lovely time, and I interposed to the effect that if I might be trusted as a tame bachelor fairly sea-seasoned, I should be delighted to give the new member of our party an arm or any other countenance whenever she should require it. Both the ladies thanked me for this—taking my professions with no sort of abatement—and the elder one declared that we were evidently going to be such a sociable group that it was too bad to have to stay at home. She asked Mrs. Nettlepoint if there were any one else in our party, and when our hostess mentioned her son—there was a chance of his embarking but (wasn't it absurd?) he hadn't decided yet—she returned with extraordinary candour: "Oh dear, I do hope he'll go: that would be so lovely for Grace."

Somehow the words made me think of poor Mr. Porterfield's tartan, especially as Jasper Nettlepoint strolled in again at that moment. His mother at once challenged him: it was ten o'clock; had he by chance made up his great mind? Apparently he failed to hear her, being in the first place surprised at the strange ladies and then struck with the fact that one of them wasn't strange. The young man, after a slight hesitation, greeted Miss Mavis with a handshake and a "Oh good-evening, how do you do?" He didn't utter her name—which I could see he must have forgotten; but she immediately pronounced his, availing herself of the American girl's discretion to "present" him to her mother.

"Well, you might have told me you knew him all this time!" that lady jovially cried. Then she had an equal confidence for Mrs. Nettlepoint. "It would have saved me a worry—an acquaintance already begun."

"Ah my son's acquaintances!" our hostess murmured.

"Yes, and my daughter's too!" Mrs. Mavis gaily echoed. "Mrs. Allen didn't tell us *you* were going," she continued to the young man.

"She'd have been clever if she had been able to!" Mrs. Nettlepoint sighed.

"Dear mother, I have my telegram," Jasper remarked, looking at Grace Mavis.

"I know you very little," the girl said, returning his observation.

"I've danced with you at some ball—for some sufferers by something or other."

"I think it was an inundation or a big fire," she a little languidly smiled. "But it was a long time ago—and I haven't seen you since."

"I've been in far countries—to my loss. I should have said it was a big fire."

"It was at the Horticultural Hall. I didn't remember your name," said Grace Mavis.

"That's very unkind of you, when I recall vividly that you had a pink dress."

"Oh I remember that dress—your strawberry tarletan: you looked lovely in it!" Mrs. Mavis broke out. "You must get another just like it—on the other side."

"Yes, your daughter looked charming in it," said Jasper Nettlepoint. Then he added to the girl: "Yet you mentioned my name to your mother."

"It came back to me—seeing you here. I had no idea this was your home."

"Well, I confess it isn't, much. Oh there are some drinks!"—he approached the tray and its glasses.

"Indeed there are and quite delicious"—Mrs. Mavis largely wiped her mouth.

"Won't you have another then?—a pink one, like your daughter's gown."

"With pleasure, sir. Oh do see them over," Mrs. Mavis continued, accepting from the young man's hand a third tumbler.

"My mother and that gentleman? Surely they can take care of themselves," he freely pleaded.

"Then my daughter—she has a claim as an old friend."

But his mother had by this time interposed. "Jasper, what does your telegram say?"

He paid her no heed: he stood there with his glass in his hand, looking from Mrs. Mavis to Miss Grace.

"Ah leave her to me, madam; I'm quite competent," I said to Mrs. Mavis.

Then the young man gave me his attention. The next minute he asked of the girl: "Do you mean you're going to Europe?"

"Yes, tomorrow. In the same ship as your mother."

"That's what we've come here for, to see all about it," said Mrs. Mavis.

"My son, take pity on me and tell me what light your telegram throws," Mrs. Nettlepoint went on.

"I will, dearest, when I've quenched my thirst." And he slowly drained his glass.

"Well, I declare you're worse than Gracie," Mrs. Mavis commented. "She was first one thing and then the other—but only about up to three o'clock yesterday."

"Excuse me—won't you take something?" Jasper inquired of Gracie; who however still declined, as if to make up for her mother's copious *consommation*. I found myself quite aware that the two ladies would do well to take leave, the question of Mrs. Nettlepoint's good will being so satisfactorily settled and the meeting of the morrow at the ship so near at hand and I went so far as to judge that their protracted stay, with their hostess visibly in a fidget, gave the last proof of their want of breeding. Miss Grace after all then was not such an improvement on her mother, for she easily might have taken the initiative of departure, in spite of Mrs. Mavis's evident "game" of making her own absorption of refreshment last as long as possible. I watched the girl with increasing interest; I couldn't help asking myself a question or two about her and even perceiving already (in a dim and general way) that rather marked embarrassment, or at least anxiety attended her. Wasn't it complicating that she should have needed, by remaining long enough, to assuage a certain suspense, to learn whether or no Jasper were going to sail? Hadn't something particular passed between them on the occasion or at the period to which we had caught their allusion, and didn't she really not know her mother was bringing her to *his* mother's, though she apparently had thought it well not to betray knowledge? Such things were symptomatic—though indeed one scarce knew of what—on the part of a young lady betrothed to that curious cross-barred phantom of a Mr. Porterfield. But I am bound to add that she gave me no further warrant for wonder than was conveyed in her all tacitly and covertly encouraging her mother to linger. Somehow I had a sense that *she* was conscious of the indecency of this. I got up myself to go, but Mrs. Nettlepoint detained me after seeing that my movement wouldn't be taken as a hint, and I felt she wished me not to leave my fellow visitors on her hands. Jasper complained of the closeness of the room, said that it was not a night to sit in a room—one ought to be out in the air, under the sky. He denounced the windows that overlooked the water for not opening upon a balcony or a terrace, until his mother, whom he hadn't yet satisfied about his telegram, reminded him that there was a beautiful balcony in front, with room for a dozen people. She assured him we would go and sit there if it would please him.

"It will be nice and cool tomorrow, when we steam into the great ocean," said Miss Mavis, expressing with more vivacity than she had yet thrown into any of her utterances my own thought of half an hour before. Mrs. Nettlepoint replied that it would probably be freezing cold, and her son murmured that he would go and try the drawing-room balcony and report upon it. Just as he was turning away he said, smiling, to Miss Mavis: "Won't you come with me and see if it's pleasant?"

"Oh well, we had better not stay all night!" her mother exclaimed, but still without moving. The girl moved, after a moment's hesitation;—she rose and accompanied Jasper to the other room. I saw how her slim tallness showed to advantage as she walked, and that she looked well as she passed, with her head thrown back, into the darkness of the other part of the house. There was something rather marked, rather surprising—I scarcely knew why, for the act in itself was simple enough—in her acceptance of such a plea, and perhaps it was our sense of this that held the rest of us somewhat stiffly silent as she remained away. I was waiting for Mrs. Mavis to go, so that I myself might go; and Mrs. Nettlepoint was waiting for her to go so that I mightn't. This doubtless made the young lady's absence appear to us longer than it really was—it was probably very brief. Her mother moreover, I think, had now a vague lapse from ease. Jasper Nettlepoint presently returned to the back drawing-room to serve his companion with our lucent syrup, and he took occasion to remark that it was lovely on the balcony: one really got some air, the breeze being from that quarter. I remembered, as he went away with his tinkling tumbler, that from *my* hand, a few minutes before, Miss Mavis had not been willing to accept this innocent offering. A little later Mrs. Nettlepoint said: "Well, if it's so pleasant there we had better go ourselves." So we passed to the front and in the other room met the two young people coming in from the balcony. I was to wonder, in the light of later things, exactly how long they had occupied together a couple of the set of cane chairs garnishing the place in summer. If it had been but five minutes that only made subsequent events more curious. "We must go, mother," Miss Mavis immediately said; and a moment after, with a little renewal of chatter as to our general meeting on the ship, the visitors had taken leave. Jasper went down with them to the door and as soon as they had got off Mrs. Nettlepoint quite richly exhaled her impression. "Ah but'll she be a bore—she'll be a bore of bores!"

"Not through talking too much, surely."

"An affectation of silence is as bad. I hate that particular *pose*; it's coming p very much now; an imitation of the English, like everything else. A girl ho tries to be statuesque at sea—that will act on one's nerves!"

"I don't know what she tries to be, but she succeeds in being very andsome."

"So much the better for you. I'll leave her to you, for I shall be shut up. like her being placed under my 'care'!" my friend cried.

"She'll be under Jasper's," I remarked.

"Ah he won't go," she wailed—"I want it too much!"

"But I didn't see it that way. I have an idea he'll go."

"Why didn't he tell me so then—when he came in?"

"He was diverted by that young woman—a beautiful unexpected girl itting there."

"Diverted from his mother and her fond hope?—his mother trembling or his decision?"

"Well"—I pieced it together—"she's an old friend, older than we know. t was a meeting after a long separation."

"Yes, such a lot of them as he does know!" Mrs. Nettlepoint sighed.

"Such a lot of them?"

"He has so many female friends—in the most varied circles."

"Well, we can close round her then," I returned; "for I on my side know, r used to know, her young man."

"Her intended?"—she had a light of relief for this.

"The very one she's going out to. He can't, by the way," it occurred to ne, "be very young now."

"How odd it sounds—her muddling after him!" said Mrs. Nettlepoint

I was going to reply that it wasn't odd if you knew Mr. Porterfield, but reflected that that perhaps only made it odder. I told my companion briefly who he was—that I had met him in the old Paris days, when I believed for a fleeting hour that I could learn to paint, when I lived with the *jeunesse de écoles*; and her comment on this was simply: "Well, he had better have come out for her!"

"Perhaps so. She looked to me as she sat there as if, she might change her mind at the last moment."

"About her marriage?"

"About sailing. But she won't change now."

Jasper came back, and his mother instantly challenged him "Well, *are* you going?"

"Yes, I shall go"—he was finally at peace about it. "I've got my telegram."

"Oh your telegram!"—I ventured a little to jeer.

"That charming girl's your telegram."

He gave me a look, but in the dusk I couldn't make out very well what it conveyed. Then he bent over his mother, kissing her. "My news isn't particularly satisfactory. I'm going for *you*."

"Oh you humbug!" she replied. But she was of course delighted.

II

PEOPLE usually spend the first hours of a voyage in squeezing themselves into their cabins, taking their little precautions, either so excessive or so inadequate, wondering how they can pass so many days in such a hole and asking idiotic questions of the stewards, who appear in comparison rare men of the world. My own initiations were rapid, as became an old sailor, and so, it seemed, were Miss Mavis's, for when I mounted to the deck at the end of half an hour I found her there alone, in the stern of the ship, her eyes on the dwindling continent. It dwindled very fast for so big a place. I accosted her, having had no conversation with her amid the crowd of leave-takers and the muddle of farewells before we put off; we talked a little about the boat, our fellow-passengers and our prospects, and then I said: "I think you mentioned last night a name I know—that of Mr. Porterfield."

"Oh no I didn't!" she answered very straight while she smiled at me through her closely-drawn veil.

"Then it was your mother."

"Very likely it was my mother." And she continued to smile as if I ought to have known the difference.

"I venture to allude to him because I've an idea I used to know him," I went on.

"Oh, I see." And beyond this remark she appeared to take no interest; she left it to me to make any connexion.

"That is if it's the same one." It struck me as feeble to say nothing more; so I added "My Mr. Porterfield was called David."

"Well, so is ours." "Ours" affected me as clever.

"I suppose I shall see him again if he's to meet you at Liverpool," I continued.

"Well, it will be bad if he doesn't."

It was too soon for me to have the idea that it would be bad if he did: that only came later. So I remarked that, not having seen him for so many years, it was very possible I shouldn't know him.

"Well, I've not seen him for a considerable time, but I expect I shall know him all the same."

"Oh with you it's different," I returned with harmlessly bright significance. "Hasn't he been back since those days?"

"I don't know," she sturdily professed, "what days you mean."

"When I knew him in Paris—ages ago. He was a pupil of the École des Beaux Arts. He was studying architecture."

"Well, he's studying it still," said Grace Mavis.

"Hasn't he learned it yet?"

"I don't know what he has learned. I shall see." Then she added for the benefit of my perhaps undue levity: "Architecture's very difficult and he's tremendously thorough."

"Oh yes, I remember that. He was an admirable worker. But he must have become quite a foreigner if it's so many years since he has been at home."

She seemed to regard this proposition at first as complicated; but she did what she could for me. "Oh he's not changeable. If he were changeable—"

Then, however, she paused. I daresay she had been going to observe that if he were changeable he would long ago have given her up. After an instant she went on: "He wouldn't have stuck so to his profession. You can't make much by it."

I sought to attenuate her rather odd maidenly grimness. "It depends on what you call much."

"It doesn't make you rich."

"Oh of course you've got to practise it—and to practise it long."

"Yes—so Mr. Porterfield says."

Something in the way she uttered these words made me laugh—they were so calm an implication that the gentleman in question didn't live up to his principles. But I checked myself, asking her if she expected to remain in Europe long—to what one might call settle.

"Well, it will be a good while if it takes me as long to come back as it has taken me to go out."

"And I think your mother said last night that it was your first visit."

Miss Mavis, in her deliberate way, met my eyes. "Didn't mother talk!"

"It was all very interesting."

She continued to look at me. "You don't think that," she then simply stated.

"What have I to gain then by saying it?"

"Oh men have always something to gain."

"You make me in that case feel a terrible failure! I hope at any rate that it gives you pleasure," I went on, "the idea of seeing foreign lands."

"Mercy—I should think so!"

This was almost genial, and it cheered me proportionately. "It's a pity our ship's not one of the fast ones, if you're impatient."

She was silent a little after which she brought out: "Oh I guess it'll be fast enough!"

That evening I went in to see Mrs. Nettlepoint and sat on her sea-trunk, which was pulled out from under the berth to accommodate me. It was nine o'clock but not quite dark, as our northward course had already taken us into the latitude of the longer days. She had made her nest admirably and now rested from her labours; she lay upon her sofa in a dressing-gown and a cap that became her. It was her regular practice to spend the voyage in her cabin, which smelt positively good—such was the refinement of her art; and she had a secret peculiar to herself for keeping her port open without shipping seas. She hated what she called the mess of the ship and the idea, if she should go above, of meeting stewards with plates of supererogatory food. She professed to be content with her situation—we promised to lend each other books and I assured her familiarly that I should be in and out of her room a dozen times a day—pitying me for having to mingle in society. She judged this a limited privilege, for on the deck before we left the wharf she had taken a view of our fellow-passengers.

"Oh I'm an inveterate, almost a professional observer," I replied, "and with that vice I'm as well occupied as an old woman in the sun with her knitting. It makes me, in any situation, just inordinately and submissively *see* things. I shall see them even here and shall come down very often and tell you about them. You're not interested today, but you will be tomorrow, for a ship's a great school of gossip. You won't believe the number of researches and problems you'll be engaged in by the middle of the voyage."

"I? Never in the world!—lying here with my nose in a book and not caring a straw."

"You'll participate at second hand. You'll see through my eyes, hang upon my lips, take sides, feel passions, all sorts of sympathies and indignations. I've an idea," I further developed, "that your young lady's the person on board who will interest me most."

"'Mine' indeed! She hasn't been near me since we left the dock."

"There you are—you do feel she owes you something. Well," I added, "she's very curious."

"You've such cold-blooded terms!" Mrs. Nettlepoint wailed. "Elle ne sait pas se conduire; she ought to have come to ask about me."

"Yes, since you're under her care," I laughed. "As for her not knowing how to behave—well, that's exactly what we shall see."

"You will, but not I! I wash my hands of her."

"Don't say that—don't say that."

Mrs. Nettlepoint looked at me a moment. "Why do you speak so solemnly?"

In return I considered her. "I'll tell you before we land. And have you seen much of your son?"

"Oh yes, he has come in several times. He seems very much pleased. He has got a cabin to himself."

"That's great luck," I said, "but I've an idea he's always in luck. I was sure I should have to offer him the second berth in my room."

"And you wouldn't have enjoyed that, because you don't like him," she took upon herself to say.

"What put that into your head?"

"It isn't in my head—it's in my heart, my *cœur de mère*. We guess those things. You think he's selfish. I could see it last night."

"Dear lady," I contrived promptly enough to reply, "I've no general ideas about him at all. He's just one of the phenomena I am going to observe. He seems to me a very fine young man. However," I added, "since you've mentioned last night I'll admit that I thought he rather tantalised you. He played with your suspense."

"Why he came at the last just to please me," said Mrs. Nettlepoint.

I was silent a little. "Are you sure it was for your sake?"

"Ah, perhaps it was for yours!"

I bore up, however, against this thrust, characteristic of perfidious woman when you presume to side with her against a fond tormentor. "When he went out on the balcony with that girl," I found assurance to suggest, "perhaps she asked him to come for *hers*."

"Perhaps she did. But why should he do everything she asks him—such as she is?"

"I don't know yet, but perhaps I shall know later. Not that he'll tell me—for he'll never tell me anything: he's not," I consistently opined, "one of those who tell."

"If she didn't ask him, what you say is a great wrong to her," said Mrs. Nettlepoint.

"Yes, if she didn't. But you say that to protect Jasper—not to protect her," I smiled.

"You *are* cold-blooded—it's uncanny!" my friend exclaimed.

"Ah this is nothing yet! Wait a while—you'll see. At sea in general I'm awful—I exceed the limits. If I've outraged her in thought I'll jump overboard. There are ways of asking—a man doesn't need to tell a woman that—without the crude words."

"I don't know what you imagine between them," said Mrs. Nettlepoint.

"Well, nothing," I allowed, "but what was visible on the surface. It transpired, as the newspapers say, that they were old friends."

"He met her at some promiscuous party—I asked him about it afterwards. She's not a person"—my hostess was confident—"whom he could ever think of seriously."

"That's exactly what I believe."

"You don't observe—you know—you imagine," Mrs. Nettlepoint continued to argue. "How do you reconcile her laying a trap for Jasper with her going out to Liverpool on an errand of love?"

Oh I wasn't to be caught that way! "I don't for an instant suppose she laid a trap; I believe she acted on the impulse of the moment. She's going out to Liverpool on an errand of marriage; that's not necessarily the same thing as an errand of love, especially for one who happens to have had a personal impression of the gentleman she's engaged to."

"Well, there are certain decencies which in such a situation the most abandoned of her sex would still observe. You apparently judge her capable—on no evidence—of violating them."

"Ah you don't understand the shades of things," I returned. "Decencies and violations, dear lady—there's no need for such heavy artillery! I can perfectly imagine that without the least immodesty she should have said to Jasper on the balcony, in fact if not in words: 'I'm in dreadful spirits, but if you come I shall feel better, and that will be pleasant for you too.'"

"And why is she in dreadful spirits?"

"She isn't!" I replied, laughing.

My poor friend wondered. "What then is she doing?"

"She's walking with your son."

Mrs. Nettlepoint for a moment said nothing; then she treated me to another inconsequence. "Ah she's horrid!"

"No, she's charming!" I protested.

"You mean she's 'curious'?"

"Well, for me it's the same thing!"

This led my friend of course to declare once more that I was cold-blooded. On the afternoon of the morrow we had another talk, and she told me that in the morning Miss Mavis had paid her a long visit. She knew nothing, poor creature, about anything, but her intentions were good and she was evidently in her own eyes conscientious and decorous. And Mrs. Nettlepoint concluded these remarks with the sigh "Unfortunate person!"

"You think she's a good deal to be pitied then?"

"Well, her story sounds dreary—she told me a good deal of it. She fell to talking little by little and went from one thing to another. She's in that situation when a girl *must* open herself—to some woman."

"Hasn't she got Jasper?" I asked.

"He isn't a woman. You strike me as jealous of him," my companion added.

"I daresay *he* thinks so—or will before the end. Ah no—ah no!" And I asked Mrs. Nettlepoint if our young lady struck her as, very grossly, a flirt. She gave me no answer, but went on to remark that she found it odd and interesting to see the way a girl like Grace Mavis resembled the girls of the kind she herself knew better, the girls of "society," at the same time that she differed from them; and the way the differences and resemblances were so mixed up that on certain questions you couldn't tell where you'd find her. You'd think she'd feel as you did because you had found her feeling so, and then suddenly, in regard to some other matter—which was yet quite the same—she'd be utterly wanting. Mrs. Nettlepoint proceeded to observe—to such idle speculations does the vacancy of sea-hours give encouragement—that she wondered whether it were better to be an ordinary girl very well brought up or an extraordinary girl not brought up at all.

"Oh I go in for the extraordinary girl under all circumstances."

"It's true that if you're *very* well brought up you're not, you can't be, ordinary," said Mrs. Nettlepoint, smelling her strong salts. "You're a lady, at any rate."

"And Miss Mavis is fifty miles out—is that what you mean?"

"Well—you've seen her mother."

"Yes, but I think your contention would be that among such people the mother doesn't count."

"Precisely, and that's bad."

"I see what you mean. But isn't it rather hard? If your mother doesn't know anything it's better you should be independent of her, and yet if you are that constitutes a bad note." I added that Mrs. Mavis had appeared to count sufficiently two nights before. She had said and done everything she wanted, while the girl sat silent and respectful. Grace's attitude, so far as her parent was concerned, had been eminently decent.

"Yes, but she 'squirmed' for her," said Mrs. Nettlepoint.

"Ah if you know it I may confess she has told me as much."

My friend stared. "Told *you*? There's one of the things they do!"

"Well, it was only a word. Won't you let me know whether you do think her a flirt?"

"Try her yourself—that's better than asking another woman; especially as you pretend to study folk."

"Oh your judgement wouldn't probably at all determine mine. It's as bearing on *you* I ask it." Which, however, demanded explanation, so that I was duly frank; confessing myself curious as to how far maternal immorality would go.

It made her at first but repeat my words. "Maternal immorality?"

"You desire your son to have every possible distraction on his voyage, and if you can make up your mind in the sense I refer to that will make it all right. He'll have no responsibility."

"Heavens, how you analyse!" she cried. "I haven't in the least your passion for making up my mind."

"Then if you chance it," I returned, "you'll be more immoral still."

"Your reasoning's strange," said Mrs. Nettlepoint; "when it was you who tried to put into my head yesterday that she had asked him to come."

"Yes, but in good faith."

"What do you mean, in such a case, by that?"

"Why, as girls of that sort do. Their allowance and measure in such matters," I expounded, "is much larger than that of young persons who have been, as you say, *very* well brought up; and yet I'm not sure that on the whole I don't think them thereby the more innocent. Miss Mavis is engaged, and she's to be married next week, but it's an old old story, and there's no more romance in it than if she were going to be photographed. So her usual life proceeds, and her usual life consists—and that of *ces demoiselles* in general—in having plenty of gentlemen's society. Having it I mean without having any harm from it."

Mrs. Nettlepoint had given me due attention. "Well, if there's no harm from it what are you talking about and why am I immoral?"

I hesitated, laughing. "I retract—you're sane and clear. I'm sure she thinks there won't be any harm," I added. "That's the great point."

"The great point?"

"To be settled, I mean."

"Mercy, we're not trying them!" cried my friend. "How can *we* settle it?"

"I mean of course in our minds. There will be nothing more interesting these next ten days for our minds to exercise themselves upon."

"Then they'll get terribly tired of it," said Mrs. Nettlepoint.

"No, no—because the interest will increase and the plot will thicken. It simply can't *not*," I insisted. She looked at me as if she thought me more than Mephistophelean, and I went back to something she had lately mentioned. "So she told you everything in her life was dreary?"

"Not everything, but most things. And she didn't tell me so much as I guessed it. She'll tell me more the next time. She'll behave properly now about coming in to see me; I told her she ought to."

"I'm glad of that," I said. "Keep her with you as much as possible."

"I don't follow you closely," Mrs. Nettlepoint replied, "but so far as I do I don't think your remarks in the best taste."

"Well, I'm too excited, I lose my head in these sports," I had to recognise—"cold-blooded as you think me. Doesn't she like Mr. Porterfield?"

"Yes, that's the worst of it."

I kept making her stare. "The worst of it?"

"He's so good—there's no fault to be found with him. Otherwise she'd ave thrown it all up. It has dragged on since she was eighteen: she became ngaged to him before he went abroad to study. It was one of those very oung and perfectly needless blunders that parents in America might make o much less possible than they do. The thing is to insist on one's daughter aiting, on the engagement's being long; and then, after you've got that arted, to take it on every occasion as little seriously as possible—to make it ie out. You can easily tire it to death," Mrs. Nettlepoint competently stated. However," she concluded, "Mr. Porterfield has taken this one seriously for me years. He has done his part to keep it alive. She says he adores her."

"His part? Surely his part would have been to marry her by this time."

"He has really no money." My friend was even more confidently able to eport it than I had been.

"He ought to have got some, in seven years," I audibly reflected.

"So I think she thinks. There are some sorts of helplessness that are ontemptible. However, a small difference has taken place. That's why he on't wait any longer. His mother has come out, she has something—a ttle—and she's able to assist him. She'll live with them and bear some of the xpenses, and after her death the son will have what there is."

"How old is she?" I cynically asked.

"I haven't the least idea. But it doesn't, on his part, sound very heroic— r very inspiring for our friend here. He hasn't been to America since he first ent out."

"That's an odd way of adoring her," I observed.

"I made that objection mentally, but I didn't express it to her. She met it ndeed a little by telling me that he had had other chances to marry."

"That surprises me," I remarked. "But did she say," I asked, "that *she* had ad?"

"No, and that's one of the things I thought nice in her; for she must have had. She didn't try to make out that he had spoiled her life. She has three other sisters and there's very little money at home. She has tried to make money; she has written little things and painted little things—and dreadful little things they must have been; too bad to think of. Her father has had a long illness and has lost his place—he was in receipt of a salary in connexion with some waterworks—and one of her sisters has lately become a widow with children and without means. And so as in fact she never has married any one else, whatever opportunities she may have encountered, she appears to have just made up her mind to go out to Mr. Porterfield as the least of her evils. But it isn't very amusing."

"Well," I judged after all, "that only makes her doing it the more honourable. She'll go through with it, whatever it costs, rather than disappoint him after he has waited so long. It's true," I continued, "that when a woman acts from a sense of honour—!"

"Well, when she does?" said Mrs. Nettlepoint, for I hung back perceptibly.

"It's often so extravagant and unnatural a proceeding as to entail heavy costs on some one."

"You're very impertinent. We all have to pay for each other all the while and for each other's virtues as well as vices."

"That's precisely why I shall be sorry for Mr. Porterfield when she steps off the ship with her little bill. I mean with her teeth clenched."

"Her teeth are not in the least clenched. She's quite at her ease now"— Mrs. Nettlepoint could answer for that.

"Well, we must try and keep her so," I said.

"You must take care that Jasper neglects nothing." I scarce know what reflexions this innocent pleasantry of mine provoked on the good lady's part; the upshot of them at all events was to make her say: "Well, I never asked her to come; I'm very glad of that. It's all their own doing."

"'Their' own—you mean Jasper's and hers?"

"No indeed. I mean her mother's and Mrs. Allen's; the girl's too of course. They put themselves on us by main force."

"Oh yes, I can testify to that. Therefore I'm glad too. We should have missed it, I think."

"How seriously you take it!" Mrs. Nettlepoint amusedly cried.

"Ah wait a few days!"—and I got up to leave her.

III

THE *Patagonia* was slow, but spacious and comfortable, and there was a motherly decency in her long nursing rock and her rustling old-fashioned gait, the multitudinous swish, in her wake, as of a thousand proper petticoats. It was as if she wished not to present herself in port with the splashed eagerness of a young creature. We weren't numerous enough quite to elbow each other and yet weren't too few to support—with that familiarity and relief which figures and objects acquire on the great bare field of the ocean and under the great bright glass of the sky. I had never liked the sea so much before, indeed I had never liked it at all; but now I had a revelation of how in a midsummer mood it could please. It was darkly and magnificently blue and imperturbably quiet—save for the great regular swell of its heartbeats, the pulse of its life; and there grew to be something so agreeable in the sense of floating there in infinite isolation and leisure that it was a positive godsend the *Patagonia* was no racer. One had never thought of the sea as the great place of safety, but now it came over one that there's no place so safe from the land. When it doesn't confer trouble it takes trouble away—takes away letters and telegrams and newspapers and visits and duties and efforts, all the complications, all the superfluities and superstitions that we have stuffed into our terrene life. The simple absence of the post, when the particular conditions enable you to enjoy the great fact by which it's produced, becomes in itself a positive bliss, and the clean boards of the deck turn to the stage of a play that amuses, the personal drama of the voyage, the movement and interaction, in the strong sea-light, of figures that end by representing something—something moreover of which the interest is never, even in its keenness, too great to suffer you to slumber. I at any rate dozed to excess, stretched on my rug with a French novel, and when I opened my eyes I generally saw Jasper Nettlepoint pass with the young woman confided to his mother's care on his arm. Somehow at these moments, between sleeping and waking, I inconsequently felt that my French novel had set them in motion. Perhaps this was because I had fallen into the trick, at the start, of regarding Grace Mavis almost as a married woman, which, as every one knows, is the necessary status of the heroine of such a work. Every revolution of our engine at any rate would contribute to the effect of making her one.

In the saloon, at meals, my neighbour on the right was a certain little Mrs. Peck, a very short and very round person whose head was enveloped in a "cloud" (a cloud of dirty white wool) and who promptly let me know that she was going to Europe for the education of her children. I had already perceived—an hour after we left the dock—that some energetic measure was required in their interest, but as we were not in Europe yet the redemption of the four little Pecks was stayed. Enjoying untrammelled leisure they swarmed about the ship as if they had been pirates boarding her, and their mother was as powerless to check their licence as if she had been gagged and stowed away in the hold. They were especially to be trusted to dive between the legs of the stewards when these attendants arrived with bowls of soup for the languid ladies. Their mother was too busy counting over to her fellow-passengers all the years Miss Mavis had been engaged. In the blank of our common detachment things that were nobody's business very soon became everybody's, and this was just one of those facts that are propagated with mysterious and ridiculous speed. The whisper that carries them is very small, in the great scale of things, of air and space and progress, but it's also very safe, for there's no compression, no sounding-board, to make speakers responsible. And then repetition at sea is somehow not repetition; monotony is in the air, the mind is flat and everything recurs—the bells, the meals, the stewards' faces, the romp of children, the walk, the clothes, the very shoes and buttons of passengers taking their exercise. These things finally grow at once so circumstantial and so arid that, in comparison, lights on the personal history of one's companions become a substitute for the friendly flicker of the lost fireside.

Jasper Nettlepoint sat on my left hand when he was not upstairs seeing that Miss Mavis had her repast comfortably on deck. His mother's place would have been next mine had she shown herself, and then that of the young lady under her care. These companions, in other words, would have been between us, Jasper marking the limit of the party in that quarter. Miss Mavis was present at luncheon the first day, but dinner passed without her coming in, and when it was half over Jasper remarked that he would go up and look after her.

"Isn't that young lady coming—the one who was here to lunch?" Mrs. Peck asked of me as he left the saloon.

"Apparently not. My friend tells me she doesn't like the saloon."

"You don't mean to say she's sick, do you?"

"Oh no, not in this weather. But she likes to be above."

"And is that gentleman gone up to her?"

"Yes, she's under his mother's care."

"And is his mother up there, too?" asked Mrs. Peck, whose processes were homely and direct.

"No, she remains in her cabin. People have different tastes. Perhaps that's one reason why Miss Mavis doesn't come to table," I added—"her chaperon not being able to accompany her."

"Her chaperon?" my fellow passenger echoed.

"Mrs. Nettlepoint—the lady under whose protection she happens to be."

"Protection?" Mrs. Peck stared at me a moment, moving some valued morsel in her mouth; then she exclaimed familiarly "Pshaw!" I was struck with this and was on the point of asking her what she meant by it when she continued: "Ain't we going to see Mrs. Nettlepoint?"

"I'm afraid not. She vows she won't stir from her sofa."

"Pshaw!" said Mrs. Peck again. "That's quite a disappointment."

"Do you know her then?"

"No, but I know all about her." Then my companion added: "You don't mean to say she's any real relation?"

"Do you mean to me?"

"No, to Grace Mavis."

"None at all. They're very new friends, as I happen to know. Then ou're acquainted with our young lady?" I hadn't noticed the passage of any cognition between them at luncheon.

"Is she your young lady too?" asked Mrs. Peck with high significance.

"Ah when people are in the same boat—literally—they belong a little o each other."

"That's so," said Mrs. Peck. "I don't know Miss Mavis, but I know all out her—I live opposite to her on Merrimac Avenue. I don't know whether ou know that part."

"Oh yes—it's very beautiful."

The consequence of this remark was another "Pshaw!" But Mrs. Peck ent on: "When you've lived opposite to people like that for a long time you el as if you had some rights in them—tit for tat! But she didn't take it up oday; she didn't speak to me. She knows who I am as well as she knows her wn mother."

"You had better speak to her first—she's constitutionally shy," I remarked.

"Shy? She's constitutionally tough! Why she's thirty years old," cried 1y neighbour. "I suppose you know where she's going."

"Oh yes—we all take an interest in that."

"That young man, I suppose, particularly." And then as I feigned a agueness: "The handsome one who sits *there*. Didn't you tell me he's Mrs. Jettlepoint's son?"

"Oh yes—he acts as her deputy. No doubt he does all he can to carry ut her function."

Mrs. Peck briefly brooded. I had spoken jocosely, but she took it with a erious face. "Well, she might let him eat his dinner in peace!" she presently ut forth.

"Oh he'll come back!" I said, glancing at his place. The repast continue and when it was finished I screwed my chair round to leave the table. Mrs Peck performed the same movement and we quitted the saloon together Outside of it was the usual vestibule, with several seats, from which you coul descend to the lower cabins or mount to the promenade-deck. Mrs. Pec appeared to hesitate as to her course and then solved the problem by goin neither way. She dropped on one of the benches and looked up at me.

"I thought you said he'd come back."

"Young Nettlepoint? Yes, I see he didn't. Miss Mavis then has give him half her dinner."

"It's very kind of her! She has been engaged half her life."

"Yes, but that will soon be over."

"So I suppose—as quick as ever we land. Every one knows it on Merrima Avenue," Mrs. Peck pursued. "Every one there takes a great interest in it."

"Ah of course—a girl like that has many friends."

But my informant discriminated. "I mean even people who don't know her."

"I see," I went on: "she's so handsome that she attracts attention—peopl enter into her affairs."

Mrs. Peck spoke as from the commanding centre of these. "She *used* t be pretty, but I can't say I think she's anything remarkable today. Anyhow, i she attracts attention she ought to be all the more careful what she does. You had better tell her that."

"Oh it's none of my business!" I easily made out, leaving the terribl little woman and going above. This profession, I grant, was not perfectl attuned to my real idea, or rather my real idea was not quite in harmony wit my profession. The very first thing I did on reaching the deck was to notic that Miss Mavis was pacing it on Jasper Nettlepoint's arm and that whateve beauty she might have lost, according to Mrs. Peck's insinuation, she still kep enough to make one's eyes follow her. She had put on a crimson hood, which was very becoming to her and which she wore for the rest of the voyage. She walked very well, with long steps, and I remember that at this moment the sea had a gentle evening swell which made the great ship dip slowly, rhythmically, giving a movement that was graceful to graceful pedestrians and a more awkward one to the awkward. It was the loveliest hour of a fine day, the clear early evening, with the glow of the sunset in the air and a purple colour on the deep. It was always present to me that so the waters ploughed by the Homeric heroes must have looked. I became conscious on this particular occasion moreover that Grace Mavis would for the rest of the voyage be the most visible thing in one's range, the figure that would count most in the composition of groups. She couldn't help it, poor girl; nature had made her conspicuous—important, as the painters say. She paid for it by the corresponding exposure, the danger that people would, as I had said to Mrs. Peck, enter into her affairs.

Jasper Nettlepoint went down at certain times to see his mother, and I watched for one of these occasions—on the third day out—and took advantage of it to go and sit by Miss Mavis. She wore a light blue veil drawn tightly over her face, so that if the smile with which she greeted me rather lacked intensity I could account for it partly by that.

"Well, we're getting on—we're getting on," I said cheerfully, looking at the friendly twinkling sea.

"Are we going very fast?"

"Not fast, but steadily. *Ohne Hast, ohne Rast*—do you know German?"

"Well, I've studied it—some."

"It will be useful to you over there when you travel."

"Well yes, if we do. But I don't suppose we shall much. Mr. Nettlepoint says we ought," my young woman added in a moment.

"Ah of course *he* thinks so. He has been all over the world."

"Yes, he has described some of the places. They must be wonderful. I didn't know I should like it so much."

"But it isn't 'Europe' yet!" I laughed.

Well, she didn't care if it wasn't. "I mean going on this way. I could go on for ever—for ever and ever."

"Ah you know it's not always like this," I hastened to mention.

"Well, it's better than Boston."

"It isn't so good as Paris," I still more portentously noted.

"Oh I know all about Paris. There's no freshness in that. I feel as if I had been there all the time."

"You mean you've heard so much of it?"

"Oh yes, nothing else for ten years."

I had come to talk with Miss Mavis because she was attractive, but I had been rather conscious of the absence of a good topic, not feeling at liberty to revert to Mr. Porterfield. She hadn't encouraged me, when I spoke to her as we were leaving Boston, to go on with the history of my acquaintance with this gentleman; and yet now, unexpectedly, she appeared to imply—it was doubtless one of the disparities mentioned by Mrs. Nettlepoint—that he might be glanced at without indelicacy.

"I see—you mean by letters," I remarked.

"We won't live in a good part. I know enough to know that," she went on.

"Well, it isn't as if there were any very bad ones," I answered reassuringly.

"Why Mr. Nettlepoint says it's regular mean."

"And to what does he apply that expression?"

She eyed me a moment as if I were elegant at her expense, but she answered my question. "Up there in the Batignolles. I seem to make out it's worse than Merrimac Avenue."

"Worse—in what way?"

"Why, even less where the nice people live."

"He oughtn't to say that," I returned. And I ventured to back it up. "Don't you call Mr. Porterfield a nice person?"

"Oh it doesn't make any difference." She watched me again a moment through her veil, the texture of which gave her look a suffused prettiness. "Do you know him very little?" she asked.

"Mr. Porterfield?"

"No, Mr. Nettlepoint."

"Ah very little. He's very considerably my junior, you see."

She had a fresh pause, as if almost again for my elegance; but she went on: "He's younger than me too." I don't know what effect of the comic there could have been in it, but the turn was unexpected and it made me laugh. Neither do I know whether Miss Mavis took offence at my sensibility on this head, though I remember thinking at the moment with compunction that it had brought a flush to her cheek. At all events she got up, gathering her shawl and her books into her arm. "I'm going down—I'm tired."

"Tired of me, I'm afraid."

"No, not yet."

"I'm like you," I confessed. "I should like it to go on and on."

She had begun to walk along the deck to the companionway and I went with her. "Well, I guess *I* wouldn't, after all!"

I had taken her shawl from her to carry it, but at the top of the steps that led down to the cabins I had to give it back. "Your mother would be glad if she could know," I observed as we parted.

But she was proof against my graces. "If she could know what?"

"How well you're getting on." I refused to be discouraged. "And that good Mrs. Allen."

"Oh mother, mother! She made me come, she pushed me off." And almost as if not to say more she went quickly below.

I paid Mrs. Nettlepoint a morning visit after luncheon and another in the evening, before she "turned in." That same day, in the evening, she said to me suddenly: "Do you know what I've done? I've asked Jasper."

"Asked him what?"

"Why, if *she* asked him, you understand."

I wondered. "*Do* I understand?"

"If you don't it's because you 'regular' won't, as she says. If that girl really asked him—on the balcony—to sail with us."

"My dear lady, do you suppose that if she did he'd tell you?"

She had to recognise my acuteness. "That's just what he says. But he says she didn't."

"And do you consider the statement valuable?" I asked, laughing out. "You had better ask your young friend herself."

Mrs. Nettlepoint stared. "I couldn't do that."

On which I was the more amused that I had to explain I was only amused. "What does it signify now?"

"I thought you thought everything signified. You were so full," she cried, "of signification!"

"Yes, but we're further out now, and somehow in mid-ocean everything becomes absolute."

"What else *can* he do with decency?" Mrs. Nettlepoint went on. "If, as my son, he were never to speak to her it would be very rude and you'd think that stranger still. Then *you* would do what he does, and where would be the difference?"

"How do you know what he does? I haven't mentioned him for twenty-four hours."

"Why, she told me herself. She came in this afternoon."

"What an odd thing to tell you!" I commented.

"Not as she says it. She says he's full of attention, perfectly devoted—looks after her all the time. She seems to want me to know it, so that I may approve him for it."

"That's charming; it shows her good conscience."

"Yes, or her great cleverness."

Something in the tone in which Mrs. Nettlepoint said this caused me to return in real surprise: "Why what do you suppose she has in her mind?"

"To get hold of him, to make him go so far he can't retreat. To marry him perhaps."

"To marry him? And what will she do with Mr. Porterfield?"

"She'll ask me just to make it all right to him—or perhaps you."

"Yes, as an old friend"—and for a moment I felt it awkwardly possible. But I put to her seriously: "*Do* you see Jasper caught like that?"

"Well, he's only a boy—he's younger at least than she."

"Precisely; she regards him as a child. She remarked to me herself today, that is, that he's so much younger."

Mrs. Nettlepoint took this in. "Does she talk of it with you? That shows she has a plan, that she has thought it over!"

I've sufficiently expressed—for the interest of my anecdote—that I found an oddity in one of our young companions, but I was far from judging her capable of laying a trap for the other. Moreover my reading of Jasper wasn't in the least that he was catchable—could be made to do a thing if he didn't want to do it. Of course it wasn't impossible that he might be inclined, that he might take it—or already have taken it—into his head to go further with his mother's charge; but to believe this I should require still more proof than his always being with her. He wanted at most to "take up with her" for the voyage. "If you've questioned him perhaps you've tried to make him fee responsible," I said to my fellow critic.

"A little, but it's very difficult. Interference makes him perverse. On has to go gently. Besides, it's too absurd—think of her age. If she can't tak care of herself!" cried Mrs. Nettlepoint.

"Yes, let us keep thinking of her age, though it's not so prodigious. An if things get very bad you've one resource left," I added.

She wondered. "To lock her up in her cabin?"

"No—to come out of yours."

"Ah never, never! If it takes that to save her she must be lost. Besides what good would it do? If I were to go above she could come below."

"Yes, but you could keep Jasper with you."

"*Could* I?" Mrs. Nettlepoint demanded in the manner of a woman who knew her son.

In the saloon the next day, after dinner, over the red cloth of the tables beneath the swinging lamps and the racks of tumblers, decanters and wine glasses, we sat down to whist, Mrs. Peck, to oblige, taking a hand in the game She played very badly and talked too much, and when the rubber was over assuaged her discomfiture (though not mine—we had been partners) with a Welsh rabbit and a tumbler of something hot. We had done with the cards but while she waited for this refreshment she sat with her elbows on the table shuffling a pack.

"She hasn't spoken to me yet—she won't do it," she remarked in a moment.

"Is it possible there's any one on the ship who hasn't spoken to you?"

"Not that girl—she knows too well!" Mrs. Peck looked round our little circle with a smile of intelligence—she had familiar communicative eyes Several of our company had assembled, according to the wont, the last thing in the evening, of those who are cheerful at sea, for the consumption of grilled sardines and devilled bones.

"What then does she know?"

"Oh she knows *I* know."

"Well, we know what Mrs. Peck knows," one of the ladies of the group observed to me with an air of privilege.

"Well, you wouldn't know if I hadn't told you—from the way she acts," said our friend with a laugh of small charm.

"She's going out to a gentleman who lives over there—he's waiting there to marry her," the other lady went on, in the tone of authentic information. I remember that her name was Mrs. Gotch and that her mouth looked always as if she were whistling.

"Oh he knows—I've told him," said Mrs. Peck.

"Well, I presume every one knows," Mrs. Gotch contributed.

"Dear madam, is it every one's business?" I asked.

"Why, don't you think it's a peculiar way to act?"—and Mrs. Gotch was evidently surprised at my little protest.

"Why it's right there—straight in front of you, like a play at the theatre—as if you had paid to see it," said Mrs. Peck. "If you don't call it public!"

"Aren't you mixing things up? What do you call public?"

"Why the way they go on. They're up there now."

"They cuddle up there half the night," said Mrs. Gotch. "I don't know when they come down. Any hour they like. When all the lights are out they're up there still."

"Oh you can't tire them out. They don't want relief—like the ship's watch!" laughed one of the gentlemen.

"Well, if they enjoy each other's society what's the harm?" another asked. "They'd do just the same on land."

"They wouldn't do it on the public streets, I presume," said Mrs. Peck. "And they wouldn't do it if Mr. Porterfield was round!"

"Isn't that just where your confusion comes in?" I made answer. "It's public enough that Miss Mavis and Mr. Nettlepoint are always together, but it isn't in the least public that she's going to be married."

"Why how can you say—when the very sailors know it! The Captain knows it and all the officers know it. They see them there, especially at night, when they're sailing the ship."

"I thought there was some rule—!" submitted Mrs. Gotch.

"Well, there is—that you've got to behave yourself," Mrs. Peck explained. "So the Captain told me—he said they have some rule. He said they have to have, when people are too undignified."

"Is that the term he used?" I inquired.

"Well, he may have said when they attract too much attention."

I ventured to discriminate. "It's we who attract the attention—by talking about what doesn't concern us and about what we really don't know."

"She said the Captain said he'd tell on her as soon as ever we arrive," Mrs. Gotch none the less serenely pursued.

"*She* said—?" I repeated, bewildered.

"Well, he did say so, that he'd think it his duty to inform Mr. Porterfield when he comes on to meet her—if they keep it up in the same way," said Mrs. Peck.

"Oh they'll keep it up, don't you fear!" one of the gentlemen exclaimed.

"Dear madam, the Captain's having his joke on you," was, however, my own congruous reply.

"No, he ain't—he's right down scandalised. He says he regards us all as a real family and wants the family not to be downright coarse." I felt Mrs. Peck irritated by my controversial tone: she challenged me with considerable spirit. "How can you say I don't know it when all the street knows it and has known it for years—for years and years?" She spoke as if the girl had been engaged at least for twenty. "What's she going out for if not to marry him?"

"Perhaps she's going to see how he looks," suggested one of the gentlemen.

"He'd look queer—if he knew."

"Well, I guess he'll know," said Mrs. Gotch.

"She'd tell him herself—she wouldn't be afraid," the gentleman went on.

"Well she might as well kill him. He'll jump overboard," Mrs. Peck could foretell.

"Jump overboard?" cried Mrs. Gotch as if she hoped then that Mr. Porterfield would be told.

"He has just been waiting for this—for long, long years," said Mrs. Peck.

"Do you happen to know him?" I asked.

She replied at her convenience. "No, but I know a lady who does. Are you going up?"

I had risen from my place—I had not ordered supper. "I'm going to take a turn before going to bed."

"Well then you'll see!"

Outside the saloon I hesitated, for Mrs. Peck's admonition made me feel for a moment that if I went up I should have entered in a manner into her little conspiracy. But the night was so warm and splendid that I had been intending to smoke a cigar in the air before going below, and I didn't see why I should deprive myself of this pleasure in order to seem not to mind Mrs. Peck. I mounted accordingly and saw a few figures sitting or moving about in the darkness. The ocean looked black and small, as it is apt to do at night, and the long mass of the ship, with its vague dim wings, seemed to take up a great part of it. There were more stars than one saw on land and the heavens struck one more than ever as larger than the earth. Grace Mavis and her companion were not, so far as I perceived at first, among the few passengers who lingered late, and I was glad, because I hated to hear her talked about in the manner of the gossips I had left at supper. I wished there had been some way to prevent it, but I could think of none but to recommend her privately to reconsider her rule of discretion. That would be a very delicate business, and perhaps it would be better to begin with Jasper, though that would be delicate too. At any rate one might let him know, in a friendly spirit, to how much remark he exposed the young lady—leaving this revelation to work its way upon him. Unfortunately I couldn't altogether believe that the pair were unconscious of the observation and the opinion of the passengers. They weren't boy and girl; they had a certain social perspective in their eye. I was meanwhile at any rate in no possession of the details of that behaviour which had made them—according to the version of my good friends in the saloon—a scandal to the ship; for though I had taken due note of them, as will already have been gathered, I had taken really no such ferocious, or at least such competent, note as Mrs. Peck. Nevertheless the probability was that they knew what was thought of them—what naturally would be—and simply didn't care. That made our heroine out rather perverse and even rather shameless; and yet somehow if these were her leanings I didn't dislike her for them. I don't know what strange secret excuses I found for her. I presently indeed encountered, on the spot, a need for any I might have at call, since, just as I was on the point of going below again, after several restless turns and—within the limit where smoking was allowed—as many puffs at a cigar as I cared for, I became aware of a couple of figures settled together behind one of the lifeboats that rested on the deck. They were so placed as to be visible only to a person going close to the rail and peering a little sidewise. I don't think I peered, but as I stood a moment beside the rail my eye was attracted by a dusky object that protruded beyond the boat and that I saw at a second glance to be the tail of a lady's dress. I bent forward an instant, but even then I saw very little more; that scarcely mattered however, as I easily concluded that the persons tucked away in so snug a corner were Jasper Nettlepoint and Mr. Porterfield's intended. Tucked away was the odious right expression, and I deplored the fact so betrayed for the pitiful bad taste in it. I immediately turned away, and the next moment found myself face to face with our vessel's kipper. I had already had some conversation with him—he had been so good as to invite me, as he had invited Mrs. Nettlepoint and her son and the young lady travelling with them, and also Mrs. Peck, to sit at his table—and had observed with pleasure that his seamanship had the grace, not universal in the Atlantic liners, of a fine-weather manner.

"They don't waste much time—your friends in there," he said, nodding in the direction in which he had seen me looking.

"Ah well, they haven't much to lose."

"That's what I mean. I'm told *she* hasn't."

I wanted to say something exculpatory, but scarcely knew what note to strike. I could only look vaguely about me at the starry darkness and the sea that seemed to sleep. "Well, with these splendid nights and this perfect air people are beguiled into late hours."

"Yes, we want a bit of a blow," the Captain said.

I demurred. "How much of one?"

"Enough to clear the decks!"

He was after all rather dry and he went about his business. He had made me uneasy, and instead of going below I took a few turns more. The other walkers dropped off pair by pair—they were all men—till at last I was alone. Then after a little I quitted the field. Jasper and his companion were still behind their lifeboat. Personally I greatly preferred our actual conditions, but as I went down I found myself vaguely wishing, in the interest of I scarcely knew what, unless it had been a mere superstitious delicacy, that we might have half a gale.

Miss Mavis turned out, in sea-phrase, early; for the next morning I saw her come up only a short time after I had finished my breakfast, a ceremony over which I contrived not to dawdle. She was alone and Jasper Nettlepoint, by a rare accident, was not on deck to help her. I went to meet her—she was encumbered as usual with her shawl, her sun-umbrella and a book—and laid my hands on her chair, placing it near the stern of the ship, where she liked best to be. But I proposed to her to walk a little before she sat down, and she took my arm after I had put her accessories into the chair. The deck was clear at that hour and the morning light gay; one had an extravagant sense of good omens and propitious airs. I forget what we spoke of first, but it was because I felt these things pleasantly; and not to torment my companion nor to test her, that I couldn't help exclaiming cheerfully after a moment, as I have mentioned having done the first day: "Well, we're getting on, we're getting on!"

"Oh yes, I count every hour."

"The last days always go quicker," I said, "and the last hours—!"

"Well, the last hours?" she asked; for I had instinctively checked myself.

"Oh one's so glad then that it's almost the same as if one had arrived. Yet we ought to be grateful when the elements have been so kind to us," I added. "I hope you'll have enjoyed the voyage."

She hesitated ever so little. "Yes, much more than I expected."

"Did you think it would be very bad?"

"Horrible, horrible!"

The tone of these words was strange, but I hadn't much time to reflect upon it, for turning round at that moment I saw Jasper Nettlepoint come toward us. He was still distant by the expanse of the white deck, and I couldn't help taking him in from head to foot as he drew nearer. I don't know what rendered me on this occasion particularly sensitive to the impression, but it struck me that I saw him as I had never seen him before, saw him, thanks to the intense sea-light, inside and out, in his personal, his moral totality. It was a quick, a vivid revelation; if it only lasted a moment it had a simplifying certifying effect. He was intrinsically a pleasing apparition, with his handsome young face and that marked absence of any drop in his personal arrangements which, more than any one I've ever seen, he managed to exhibit on shipboard. He had none of the appearance of wearing out old clothes that usually prevails there, but dressed quite straight, as I heard some one say. This gave him an assured, almost a triumphant air, as of a young man who would come best out of any awkwardness. I expected to feel my companion's hand loosen itself on my arm, as an indication that now she must go to him, and I was almost surprised she didn't drop me. We stopped as we met and Jasper bade us a friendly good-morning. Of course the remark that we had another lovely day was already indicated, and it led him to exclaim, in the manner of one to whom criticism came easily, "Yes, but with this sort of thing consider what one of the others would do!"

"One of the other ships?"

"We should be there now, or at any rate tomorrow."

"Well then I'm glad it isn't one of the others"—and I smiled at the young lady on my arm. My words offered her a chance to say something appreciative, and gave him one even more; but neither Jasper nor Grace Mavis took advantage of the occasion. What they did do, I noticed, was to look at each other rather fixedly an instant; after which she turned her eyes silently to the sea. She made no movement and uttered no sound, contriving to give me the sense that she had all at once become perfectly passive, that she somehow declined responsibility. We remained standing there with Jasper in front of us, and if the contact of her arm didn't suggest I should give her up, neither did it intimate that we had better pass on. I had no idea of giving her up, albeit one of the things I seemed to read just then into Jasper's countenance was a fine implication that she was his property. His eyes met mine for a moment, and it was exactly as if he had said to me "I know what you think, but I don't care a rap." What I really thought was that he was selfish beyond the limits: that was the substance of my little revelation. Youth is almost always selfish, just as it is almost always conceited, and, after all, when it's combined with health and good parts, good looks and good spirits, it has a right to be, and I easily forgive it if it be really youth. Still it's a question of degree, and what stuck out of Jasper Nettlepoint—if, of course, one had the intelligence for it—was that his egotism had a hardness, his love of his own way an avidity. These elements were jaunty and prosperous, they were accustomed to prevail. He was fond, very fond, of women; they were necessary to him—that was in his type; but he wasn't in the least in love with

Grace Mavis. Among the reflexions I quickly made this was the one that was most to the point. There was a degree of awkwardness, after a minute, in the way we were planted there, though the apprehension of it was doubtless not in the least with himself. To dissimulate my own share in it, at any rate, I asked him how his mother might be.

His answer was unexpected. "You had better go down and see."

"Not till Miss Mavis is tired of me."

She said nothing to this and I made her walk again. For some minutes she failed to speak; then, rather abruptly, she began: "I've seen you talking to that lady who sits at our table—the one who has so many children."

"Mrs. Peck? Oh yes, one has inevitably talked with Mrs. Peck."

"Do you know her very well?"

"Only as one knows people at sea. An acquaintance makes itself. It doesn't mean very much."

"She doesn't speak to me—she might if she wanted."

"That's just what she says of you—that you might speak to her."

"Oh if she's waiting for that!" said my companion with a laugh. Then she added: "She lives in our street, nearly opposite."

"Precisely. That's the reason why she thinks you coy or haughty. She has seen you so often and seems to know so much about you."

"What does she know about me?"

"Ah you must ask her—I can't tell you!"

"I don't care what she knows," said my young lady. After a moment she went on: "She must have seen I ain't very sociable." And then, "What are you laughing at?" she asked.

"Well"—my amusement was difficult to explain—"you're not very sociable, and yet somehow you are. Mrs. Peck is, at any rate, and thought that ought to make it easy for you to enter into conversation with her."

"Oh I don't care for her conversation—I know what it amounts to." I made no reply—I scarcely knew what reply to make—and the girl went on: "I know what she thinks and I know what she says." Still I was silent, but the next moment I saw my discretion had been wasted, for Miss Mavis put to me straight: "Does she make out that she knows Mr. Porterfield?"

"No, she only claims she knows a lady who knows him."

"Yes, that's it—Mrs. Jeremie. Mrs. Jeremie's an idiot!" I wasn't in a position to controvert this, and presently my young lady said she would sit down. I left her in her chair—I saw that she preferred it—and wandered to a distance. A few minutes later I met Jasper again, and he stopped of his own accord to say: "We shall be in about six in the evening of our eleventh day—they promise it."

"If nothing happens, of course."

"Well, what's going to happen?"

"That's just what I'm wondering!" And I turned away and went below with the foolish but innocent satisfaction of thinking I had mystified him.

IV

"I DON'T know what to do, and you must help me," Mrs. Nettlepoint said to me, that evening, as soon as I looked in.

"I'll do what I can—but what's the matter?"

"She has been crying here and going on—she has quite upset me."

"Crying? She doesn't look like that."

"Exactly, and that's what startled me. She came in to see me this afternoon, as she has done before, and we talked of the weather and the run of the ship and the manners of the stewardess and other such trifles, and then suddenly, in the midst of it, as she sat there, on no visible pretext, she burst into tears. I asked her what ailed her and tried to comfort her, but she didn't explain; she said it was nothing, the effect of the sea, of the monotony, of the excitement, of leaving home. I asked her if it had anything to do with her prospects, with her marriage; whether she finds as this draws near that her heart isn't in it. I told her she mustn't be nervous, that I could enter into that—in short I said what I could. All she replied was that she *is* nervous, very nervous, but that it was already over; and then she jumped up and kissed me and went away. Does she look as if she has been crying?" Mrs. Nettlepoint wound up.

"How can I tell, when she never quits that horrid veil? It's as if she were ashamed to show her face."

"She's keeping it for Liverpool. But I don't like such incidents," said Mrs. Nettlepoint. "I think I ought to go above."

"And is that where you want me to help you?"

"Oh with your arm and that sort of thing, yes. But I may have to look to you for something more. I feel as if something were going to happen."

"That's exactly what I said to Jasper this morning."

"And what did he say?"

"He only looked innocent—as if he thought I meant a fog or a storm."

"Heaven forbid—it isn't that! I shall never be good-natured again," Mrs. Nettlepoint went on; "never have a girl put on me that way. You always pay for it—there are always tiresome complications. What I'm afraid of is after we get there. She'll throw up her engagement; there will be dreadful scenes; I shall be mixed up with them and have to look after her and keep her with me. I shall have to stay there with her till she can be sent back, or even take her up to London. Do you see all that?"

I listened respectfully; after which I observed: "You're afraid of your son."

She also had a pause. "It depends on how you mean it."

"There are things you might say to him—and with your manner; because you have one, you know, when you choose."

"Very likely, but what's my manner to his? Besides, I *have* said everything to him. That is I've said the great thing—that he's making her immensely talked about."

"And of course in answer to that he has asked you how you know, and you've told him you have it from me."

"I've had to tell him; and he says it's none of your business."

"I wish he'd say that," I remarked, "to my face."

"He'll do so perfectly if you give him a chance. That's where you can help me. Quarrel with him—he's rather good at a quarrel; and that will divert him and draw him off."

"Then I'm ready," I returned, "to discuss the matter with him for the rest of the voyage."

"Very well; I count on you. But he'll ask you, as he asks me, what the deuce you want him to do."

"To go to bed!"—and I'm afraid I laughed.

"Oh it isn't a joke."

I didn't want to be irritating, but I made my point. "That's exactly wha I told you at first."

"Yes, but don't exult; I hate people who exult. Jasper asks of me," sh went on, "why he should mind her being talked about if she doesn't mind i herself."

"I'll tell him why," I replied; and Mrs. Nettlepoint said she should b exceedingly obliged to me and repeated that she would indeed take the field

I looked for Jasper above that same evening, but circumstances didn favour my quest. I found him—that is I gathered he was again ensconce behind the lifeboat with Miss Mavis; but there was a needless violence i breaking into their communion, and I put off our interview till the next day Then I took the first opportunity, at breakfast, to make sure of it. He was i the saloon when I went in and was preparing to leave the table; but I stoppe him and asked if he would give me a quarter of an hour on deck a little later— there was something particular I wanted to say to him. He said "Oh yes, i you like"—with just a visible surprise, but I thought with plenty of assurance When I had finished my breakfast I found him smoking on the forward-deck and I immediately began: "I'm going to say something you won't at all like; t ask you a question you'll probably denounce for impertinent."

"I certainly shall if I find it so," said Jasper Nettlepoint.

"Well, of course my warning has meant that I don't care if you do. I'm good deal older than you and I'm a friend—of many years—of your mother There's nothing I like less than to be meddlesome, but I think these thing give me a certain right—a sort of privilege. Besides which my inquiry wil speak for itself."

"Why so many damned preliminaries?" my young man asked throug his smoke.

We looked into each other's eyes a moment. What indeed was his mother's manner—her best manner—compared with his? "Are you prepared to be responsible?"

"To you?"

"Dear no—to the young lady herself. I'm speaking of course of Miss Mavis."

"Ah yes, my mother tells me you have her greatly on your mind."

"So has your mother herself—now."

"She's so good as to say so—to oblige you."

"She'd oblige me a great deal more by reassuring me. I know perfectly of your knowing I've told her that Miss Mavis is greatly talked about."

"Yes, but what on earth does it matter?"

"It matters as a sign."

"A sign of what?"

"That she's in a false position."

Jasper puffed his cigar with his eyes on the horizon, and I had, a little unexpectedly, the sense of producing a certain effect on him. "I don't know whether it's *your* business, what you're attempting to discuss but it really strikes me it's none of mine. What have I to do with the tattle with which a pack of old women console themselves for not being sea-sick?"

"Do you call it tattle that Miss Mavis is in love with you?"

"Drivelling."

"Then," I retorted, "you're very ungrateful. The tattle of a pack of old women has this importance, that she suspects, or she knows, it exists, and that decent girls are for the most part very sensitive to that sort of thing. To be prepared not to heed it in this case she must have a reason, and the reason must be the one I've taken the liberty to call your attention to."

"In love with me in six days, just like that?"—and he still looked away through narrowed eyelids.

"There's no accounting for tastes, and six days at sea are equivalent to sixty on land. I don't want to make you too proud. Of course if you recognise your responsibility it's all right and I've nothing to say."

"I don't see what you mean," he presently returned.

"Surely you ought to have thought of that by this time. She's engaged to be married, and the gentleman she's engaged to is to meet her at Liverpool. The whole ship knows it—though *I* didn't tell them!—and the whole ship's watching her. It's impertinent if you like, just as I am myself, but we make a little world here together and we can't blink its conditions. What I ask you is whether you're prepared to allow her to give up the gentleman I've just mentioned for your sake."

Jasper spoke in a moment as if he didn't understand. "For my sake?"

"To marry her if she breaks with him."

He turned his eyes from the horizon to my own, and I found a strange expression in them. "Has Miss Mavis commissioned you to go into that?"

"Not in the least."

"Well then, I don't quite see—!"

"It isn't as from another I make it. Let it come from yourself—*to* yourself."

"Lord, you must think I lead myself a life!" he cried as in compassion for my simplicity. "That's a question the young lady may put to me any moment it pleases her."

"Let me then express the hope that she will. But what will you answer?"

"My dear sir, it seems to me that in spite of all the titles you've enumerated you've no reason to expect I'll tell you." He turned away, and I dedicated in perfect sincerity a deep sore sigh to the thought of our young woman. At this, under the impression of it, he faced me again and, looking at me from head to foot, demanded: "What is it you want me to do?"

"I put it to your mother that you ought to go to bed."

"You had better do that yourself!" he replied.

This time he walked off, and I reflected rather dolefully that the only clear result of my undertaking would probably have been to make it vivid to him that she was in love with him. Mrs. Nettlepoint came up as she had announced, but the day was half over: it was nearly three o'clock. She was accompanied by her son, who established her on deck, arranged her chair and her shawls, saw she was protected from sun and wind, and for an hour was very properly attentive. While this went on Grace Mavis was not visible, nor did she reappear during the whole afternoon. I hadn't observed that she had as yet been absent from the deck for so long a period. Jasper left his mother, but came back at intervals to see how she got on, and when she asked where Miss Mavis might be answered that he hadn't the least idea. I sat with my friend at her particular request: she told me she knew that if I didn't Mrs. Peck and Mrs. Gotch would make their approach, so that I must act as a watchdog. She was flurried and fatigued with her migration, and I think that Grace Mavis's choosing this occasion for retirement suggested to her a little that she had been made a fool of. She remarked that the girl's not being there showed her for the barbarian she only could be, and that she herself was really very good so to have put herself out; her charge was a mere bore: that was the end of it. I could see that my companion's advent quickened the speculative activity of the other ladies they watched her from the opposite side of the deck, keeping their eyes fixed on her very much as the man at the wheel kept his on the course of the ship. Mrs. Peck plainly had designs, and it was from this danger that Mrs. Nettlepoint averted her face.

"It's just as we said," she remarked to me as we sat there. "It's like the buckets in the well. When I come up everything else goes down."

"No, not at all everything else—since Jasper remains here."

"Remains? I don't see him."

"He comes and goes—it's the same thing."

"He goes more than he comes. But *n'en parlons plus*; I haven't gained anything. I don't admire the sea at all—what is it but a magnified water-tank? I shan't come up again."

"I've an idea she'll stay in her cabin now," I said. "She tells me she has one to herself." Mrs. Nettlepoint replied that she might do as she liked, and I repeated to her the little conversation I had had with Jasper.

She listened with interest, but "Marry her? Mercy!" she exclaimed. "I like the fine freedom with which you give my son away."

"You wouldn't accept that?"

"Why in the world should I?"

"Then I don't understand your position."

"Good heavens, I *have* none! It isn't a position to be tired of the whole thing."

"You wouldn't accept it even in the case I put to him—that of her believing she had been encouraged to throw over poor Porterfield?"

"Not even—not even. Who can know what she believes?"

It brought me back to where we had started from. "Then you do exactly what I said you would—you show me a fine example of maternal immorality."

"Maternal fiddlesticks! It was she who began it."

"Then why did you come up today?" I asked.

"To keep you quiet."

Mrs. Nettlepoint's dinner was served on deck, but I went into the saloon. Jasper was there, but not Grace Mavis, as I had half-expected. I sought to learn from him what had become of her, if she were ill—he must have thought I had an odious pertinacity—and he replied that he knew nothing whatever about her. Mrs. Peck talked to me—or tried to—of Mrs.

Nettlepoint, expatiating on the great interest it had been to see her; only it was a pity she didn't seem more sociable. To this I made answer that she was to be excused on the score of health.

"You don't mean to say she's sick on this pond?"

"No, she's unwell in another way."

"I guess I know the way!" Mrs. Peck laughed. And then she added: "I suppose she came up to look after her pet."

"Her pet?" I set my face.

"Why Miss Mavis. We've talked enough about that."

"Quite enough. I don't know what that has had to do with it. Miss Mavis, so far as I've noticed, hasn't been above today."

"Oh it goes on all the same."

"It goes on?"

"Well, it's too late."

"Too late?"

"Well, you'll see. There'll be a row."

This wasn't comforting, but I didn't repeat it on deck. Mrs. Nettlepoint returned early to her cabin, professing herself infinitely spent. I didn't know what "went on," but Grace Mavis continued not to show. I looked in late, for good-night to my friend, and learned from her that the girl hadn't been to her. She had sent the stewardess to her room for news, to see if she were ill and needed assistance, and the stewardess had come back with mere mention of her not being there. I went above after this; the night was not quite so fair and the deck almost empty. In a moment Jasper Nettlepoint and our young lady moved past me together. "I hope you're better!" I called after her; and she tossed me over her shoulder—"Oh yes, I had a headache; but the air now does me good!"

I went down again—I was the only person there but they, and I wanted not to seem to dog their steps—and, returning to Mrs. Nettlepoint's room, found (her door was open to the little passage) that she was still sitting up.

"She's all right!" I said. "She's on the deck with Jasper."

The good lady looked up at me from her book. "I didn't know you called that all right."

"Well, it's better than something else."

"Than what else?"

"Something I was a little afraid of." Mrs. Nettlepoint continued to look at me; she asked again what that might be. "I'll tell you when we're ashore," I said.

The next day I waited on her at the usual hour of my morning visit and found her not a little distraught. "The scenes have begun," she said, "you know I told you I shouldn't get through without them! You made me nervous last night—I haven't the least idea what you meant; but you made me horribly nervous. She came in to see me an hour ago, and I had the courage to say to her: 'I don't know why I shouldn't tell you frankly that I've been scolding my son about you.' Of course she asked what I meant by that, and I let her know. 'It seems to me he drags you about the ship too much for a girl in your position. He has the air of not remembering that you belong to some one else. There's a want of taste and even a want of respect in it.' That brought on an outbreak: she became very violent."

"Do you mean indignant?"

"Yes, indignant, and above all flustered and excited—at my presuming to suppose her relations with my son not the very simplest in the world. I might scold him as much as I liked—that was between ourselves; but she didn't see why I should mention such matters to herself. Did I think she allowed him to treat her with disrespect? That idea wasn't much of a compliment to either of them! He had treated her better and been kinder to her than most other people—there were very few on the ship who hadn't been insulting. She should be glad enough when she got off it, to her own people, to some one whom nobody would have a right to speak of. What was there in her position that wasn't perfectly natural? what was the idea of making a fuss about her position? Did I mean that she took it too easily—that she didn't think as much as she ought about Mr. Porterfield? Didn't I believe she was attached to him—didn't I believe she was just counting the hours till she saw him? That would be the happiest moment of her life. It showed how little I knew her if I thought anything else."

"All that must have been rather fine—I should have liked to hear it," I said after quite hanging on my friend's lips. "And what did you reply?"

"Oh I grovelled; I assured her that I accused her—as regards my son—of nothing worse than an excess of good nature. She helped him to pass his time—he ought to be immensely obliged. Also that it would be a very happy moment for me too when I should hand her over to Mr. Porterfield."

"And will you come up today?"

"No indeed—I think she'll do beautifully now."

I heaved this time a sigh of relief. "All's well that ends well!"

Jasper spent that day a great deal of time with his mother. She had told me how much she had lacked hitherto proper opportunity to talk over with him their movements after disembarking. Everything changes a little the last two or three days of a voyage; the spell is broken and new combinations take place. Grace Mavis was neither on deck nor at dinner, and I drew Mrs. Peck's attention to the extreme propriety with which she now conducted herself. She had spent the day in meditation and judged it best to continue to meditate.

"Ah she's afraid," said my implacable neighbour.

"Afraid of what?"

"Well, that we'll tell tales when we get there."

"Whom do you mean by 'we'?"

"Well, there are plenty—on a ship like this."

"Then I think," I returned, "we won't."

"Maybe we won't have the chance," said the dreadful little woman.

"Oh at that moment"—I spoke from a full experience—"universal geniality reigns."

Mrs. Peck however knew little of any such law. "I guess she's afraid all the same."

"So much the better!"

"Yes—so much the better!"

All the next day too the girl remained invisible, and Mrs. Nettlepoint told me she hadn't looked in. She herself had accordingly inquired by the stewardess if she might be received in Miss Mavis's own quarters, and the young lady had replied that they were littered up with things and unfit for visitors: she was packing a trunk over. Jasper made up for his devotion to his mother the day before by now spending a great deal of his time in the smoking-room. I wanted to say to him "This is much better," but I thought it wiser to hold my tongue. Indeed I had begun to feel the emotion of prospective arrival—the sense of the return to Europe always kept its intensity—and had thereby the less attention for other matters. It will doubtless appear to the critical reader that my expenditure of interest had been out of proportion to the vulgar appearances of which my story gives an account, but to this I can only reply that the event was to justify me. We sighted land, the dim yet rich coast of Ireland, about sunset, and I leaned on the bulwark and took it in. "It doesn't look like much, does it?" I heard a voice say, beside me; whereupon, turning, I found Grace Mavis at hand. Almost for the first time she had her veil up, and I thought her very pale.

"It will be more tomorrow," I said.

"Oh yes, a great deal more."

"The first sight of land, at sea, changes everything," I went on. "It always affects me as waking up from a dream. It's a return to reality."

For a moment she made me no response; then she said "It doesn't look very real yet."

"No, and meanwhile, this lovely evening, one can put it that the dream's still present."

She looked up at the sky, which had a brightness, though the light of the sun had left it and that of the stars hadn't begun. "It *is* a lovely evening."

"Oh yes, with this we shall do."

She stood some moments more, while the growing dusk effaced the line of the land more rapidly than our progress made it distinct. She said nothing more, she only looked in front of her; but her very quietness prompted me to something suggestive of sympathy and service. It was difficult indeed to strike the right note—some things seemed too wide of the mark and others too importunate. At last, unexpectedly, she appeared to give me my chance. Irrelevantly, abruptly she broke out: "Didn't you tell me you knew Mr. Porterfield?"

"Dear me, yes—I used to see him. I've often wanted to speak to you of him."

She turned her face on me and in the deepened evening I imagined her more pale. "What good would that do?"

"Why it would be a pleasure," I replied rather foolishly.

"Do you mean for you?"

"Well, yes—call it that," I smiled.

"Did you know him so well?"

My smile became a laugh and I lost a little my confidence. "You're not easy to make speeches to."

"I hate speeches!" The words came from her lips with a force that surprised me; they were loud and hard. But before I had time to wonder she went on a little differently. "Shall you know him when you see him?"

133

"Perfectly, I think." Her manner was so strange that I had to notice it in some way, and I judged the best way was jocularly; so I added: "Shan't you?"

"Oh perhaps you'll point him out!" And she walked quickly away. As I looked after her there came to me a perverse, rather a provoking consciousness of having during the previous days, and especially in speaking to Jasper Nettlepoint, interfered with her situation in some degree to her loss. There was an odd pang for me in seeing her move about alone; I felt somehow responsible for it and asked myself why I couldn't have kept my hands off. I had seen Jasper in the smoking-room more than once that day, as I passed it, and half an hour before this had observed, through the open door, that he was there. He had been with her so much that without him she now struck one as bereaved and forsaken. This was really better, no doubt, but superficially it moved—and I admit with the last inconsequence—one's pity. Mrs. Peck would doubtless have assured me that their separation was gammon: they didn't show together on deck and in the saloon, but they made it up elsewhere. The secret places on shipboard are not numerous; Mrs. Peck's "elsewhere" would have been vague, and I know not what licence her imagination took. It was distinct that Jasper had fallen off, but of course what had passed between them on this score wasn't so and could never be. Later on, through his mother, I had *his* version of that, but I may remark that I gave it no credit. Poor Mrs. Nettlepoint, on the other hand, was of course to give it all. I was almost capable, after the girl had left me, of going to my young man and saying: "After all, do return to her a little, just till we get in! It won't make any difference after we land." And I don't think it was the fear he would tell me I was an idiot that prevented me. At any rate the next time I passed the door of the smoking-room I saw he had left it. I paid my usual visit to Mrs. Nettlepoint that night, but I troubled her no further about Miss Mavis. She had made up her mind that everything was smooth and settled now, and it seemed to me I had worried her, and that she had worried herself, in sufficiency. I left her to enjoy the deepening foretaste of arrival, which had taken possession of her mind. Before turning in I went above and found more passengers on deck than I had ever seen so late. Jasper moved about among them alone, but I forbore to join him. The coast of Ireland had disappeared, but the night and the sea were perfect. On the way to my cabin, when I came

own, I met the stewardess in one of the passages, and the idea entered my
head to say to her: "Do you happen to know where Miss Mavis is?"

"Why she's in her room, sir, at this hour."

"Do you suppose I could speak to her?" It had come into my mind
to ask her why she had wanted to know of me if I should recognise Mr.
Porterfield.

"No sir," said the stewardess; "she has gone to bed."

"That's all right." And I followed the young lady's excellent example.

The next morning, while I dressed, the steward of my side of the ship
came to me as usual to see what I wanted. But the first thing he said to, me
was: "Rather a bad job, sir—a passenger missing." And while I took I scarce
now what instant chill from it, "A lady, sir," he went on—"whom I think
you knew. Poor Miss Mavis, sir."

"*Missing?*" I cried—staring at him and horror-stricken.

"She's not on the ship. They can't find her."

"Then where to God is she?"

I recall his queer face. "Well sir, I suppose you know that as well as I."

"Do you mean she has jumped overboard?"

"Some time in the night, sir—on the quiet. But it's beyond every one,
the way she escaped notice. They usually sees 'em, sir. It must have been
bout half-past two. Lord, but she was sharp, sir. She didn't so much as make
splash. They say she 'ad come against her will, sir."

I had dropped upon my sofa—I felt faint. The man went on, liking to
alk as persons of his class do when they have something horrible to tell. She
sually rang for the stewardess early, but this morning of course there had
een no ring. The stewardess had gone in all the same about eight o'clock and
ound the cabin empty. That was about an hour previous. Her things were
here in confusion—the things she usually wore when she went above. The

stewardess thought she had been a bit odd the night before, but had waited little and then gone back. Miss Mavis hadn't turned up—and she didn't turn up. The stewardess began to look for her—she hadn't been seen on deck or in the saloon. Besides, she wasn't dressed—not to show herself; all her clothes were in her room. There was another lady, an old lady, Mrs. Nettlepoint—would know her—that she was sometimes with, but the stewardess had been with *her* and knew Miss Mavis hadn't come near her that morning. She had spoken to *him* and they had taken a quiet look—they had hunted everywhere. A ship's a big place, but you did come to the end of it, and if a person wasn't there why there it was. In short an hour had passed and the young lady was not accounted for: from which I might judge if she ever would be. The watch couldn't account for her, but no doubt the fishes in the sea could—poor miserable pitiful lady! The stewardess and he had of course thought it their duty to speak at once to the Doctor, and the Doctor had spoken immediately to the Captain. The Captain didn't like it—they never did, but he'd try to keep it quiet—they always did.

By the time I succeeded in pulling myself together and getting on, after a fashion, the rest of my clothes I had learned that Mrs. Nettlepoint wouldn't yet have been told, unless the stewardess had broken it to her within the previous few minutes. Her son knew, the young gentleman on the other side of the ship—he had the other steward; my man had seen him come out of his cabin and rush above, just before he came in to me. He *had* gone above, my man was sure; he hadn't gone to the old lady's cabin. I catch again the sense of my dreadfully seeing something at that moment, catch the wild flash, under the steward's words, of Jasper Nettlepoint leaping, with a mad compunction in his young agility, over the side of the ship. I hasten to add, however, that no such incident was destined to contribute its horror to poor Grace Mavis's unwitnessed and unlighted tragic act. What followed was miserable enough, but I can only glance at it. When I got to Mrs. Nettlepoint's door she was there with a shawl about her; the stewardess had just told her and she was dashing out to come to me. I made her go back—I said I would go for Jasper. I went for him but I missed him, partly no doubt because it was really at first the Captain I was after. I found this personage and found him highly scandalised, but he gave me no hope that we were in error, and his displeasure, expressed with seamanlike strength, was a definite settlement of the question. From the deck, where I merely turned round and looked, I saw the light of another summer day, the coast of Ireland green and near and the sea of a more charming colour than it had shown at all. When I came below again Jasper had passed back; he had gone to his cabin and his mother had joined him there. He remained there till we reached Liverpool—I never saw him. His mother, after a little, at his request, left him alone. All the world went above to look at the land and chatter about our tragedy, but the poor lady spent the day, dismally enough, in her room. It seemed to me, the dreadful day, intolerably long; I was thinking so of vague, of inconceivable yet inevitable Porterfield, and of my having to face him somehow on the morrow. Now of course I knew why she had asked me if I should recognise him; she had delegated to me mentally a certain pleasant office. I gave Mrs. Peck and Mrs. Gotch a wide berth—I couldn't talk to them. I could, or at least I did a little, to Mrs. Nettlepoint, but with too many reserves for comfort on either side, since I quite felt how little it would now make for ease to mention Jasper to her. I was obliged to assume by my silence that he had had nothing to do with what had happened; and of course I never really ascertained what he *had* had to do. The secret of what passed between him and the strange girl who would have sacrificed her marriage to him on so short an acquaintance remains shut up in his breast. His mother, I know, went to his door from time to time, but he refused her admission. That evening, to be human at a venture, I requested the steward to go in and ask him if he should care to see me, and the good man returned with an answer which he candidly transmitted. "Not in the least!"—Jasper apparently was almost as scandalised as the Captain.

At Liverpool, at the dock, when we had touched, twenty people came on board and I had already made out Mr. Porterfield at a distance. He was looking up at the side of the great vessel with disappointment written—for my strained eyes—in his face; disappointment at not seeing the woman he had so long awaited lean over it and wave her handkerchief to him. Every one was looking at him, every one but she—his identity flew about in a moment—and I wondered if it didn't strike him. He used to be gaunt and angular, but had grown almost fat and stooped a little. The interval between us diminished—he was on the plank and then on the deck with the jostling agents of the Customs; too soon for my equanimity. I met him instantly, however, to save him from exposure—laid my hand on him and drew him away, though I was sure he had no impression of having seen me before. It was not till afterwards that I thought this rather characteristically dull of him. I drew him far away—I was conscious of Mrs. Peck and Mrs. Gotch, looking at us as we passed—into the empty stale smoking-room: he remained speechless, and that struck me as like him. I had to speak first, he couldn't even relieve me by saying "Is anything the matter?" I broke ground by putting it, feebly, that she was ill. It was a dire moment.

About Author

Henry James OM (15 April 1843 – 28 February 1916) was an merican-British author regarded as a key transitional figure between literary alism and literary modernism, and is considered by many to be among the reatest novelists in the English language. He was the son of Henry James Sr. nd the brother of renowned philosopher and psychologist William James nd diarist Alice James.

He is best known for a number of novels dealing with the social and arital interplay between émigré Americans, English people, and continental uropeans. Examples of such novels include The Portrait of a Lady, The mbassadors, and The Wings of the Dove. His later works were increasingly xperimental. In describing the internal states of mind and social dynamics f his characters, James often made use of a style in which ambiguous or ontradictory motives and impressions were overlaid or juxtaposed in the iscussion of a character's psyche. For their unique ambiguity, as well as for ther aspects of their composition, his late works have been compared to npressionist painting.

His novella The Turn of the Screw has garnered a reputation as the most nalysed and ambiguous ghost story in the English language and remains his ost widely adapted work in other media. He also wrote a number of other ighly regarded ghost stories and is considered one of the greatest masters of e field.

James published articles and books of criticism, travel, biography, utobiography, and plays. Born in the United States, James largely relocated Europe as a young man and eventually settled in England, becoming a ritish subject in 1915, one year before his death. James was nominated for e Nobel Prize in Literature in 1911, 1912 and 1916.

Life

Early years, 1843–1883

James was born at 2 Washington Place in New York City on 15 April 1843. His parents were Mary Walsh and Henry James Sr. His father was intelligent and steadfastly congenial. He was a lecturer and philosopher who had inherited independent means from his father, an Albany banker and investor. Mary came from a wealthy family long settled in New York City. Her sister Katherine lived with her adult family for an extended period of time. Henry Jr. had three brothers, William, who was one year his senior, and younger brothers Wilkinson (Wilkie) and Robertson. His younger sister was Alice. Both of his parents were of Irish and Scottish descent.

The family first lived in Albany, at 70 N. Pearl St., and then moved to Fourteenth Street in New York City when James was still a young boy. His education was calculated by his father to expose him to many influences, primarily scientific and philosophical; it was described by Percy Lubbock, the editor of his selected letters, as "extraordinarily haphazard and promiscuous." James did not share the usual education in Latin and Greek classics. Between 1855 and 1860, the James' household traveled to London, Paris, Geneva, Boulogne-sur-Mer and Newport, Rhode Island, according to the father's current interests and publishing ventures, retreating to the United States when funds were low. Henry studied primarily with tutors and briefly attended schools while the family traveled in Europe. Their longest stays were in France, where Henry began to feel at home and became fluent in French. He was afflicted with a stutter, which seems to have manifested itself only when he spoke English; in French, he did not stutter.

In 1860 the family returned to Newport. There Henry became a friend of the painter John La Farge, who introduced him to French literature, and in particular, to Balzac. James later called Balzac his "greatest master," and said that he had learned more about the craft of fiction from him than from anyone else.

In the autumn of 1861 Henry received an injury, probably to his back, while fighting a fire. This injury, which resurfaced at times throughout his life, made him unfit for military service in the American Civil War.

In 1864 the James family moved to Boston, Massachusetts to be near William, who had enrolled first in the Lawrence Scientific School at Harvard and then in the medical school. In 1862 Henry attended Harvard Law School, but realised that he was not interested in studying law. He pursued his interest in literature and associated with authors and critics William Dean Howells and Charles Eliot Norton in Boston and Cambridge, formed lifelong friendships with Oliver Wendell Holmes Jr., the future Supreme Court Justice, and with James and Annie Fields, his first professional mentors.

His first published work was a review of a stage performance, "Miss Maggie Mitchell in Fanchon the Cricket," published in 1863. About a year later, A Tragedy of Error, his first short story, was published anonymously. James's first payment was for an appreciation of Sir Walter Scott's novels, written for the North American Review. He wrote fiction and non-fiction pieces for The Nation and Atlantic Monthly, where Fields was editor. In 1871 he published his first novel, Watch and Ward, in serial form in the Atlantic Monthly. The novel was later published in book form in 1878.

During a 14-month trip through Europe in 1869–70 he met Ruskin, Dickens, Matthew Arnold, William Morris, and George Eliot. Rome impressed him profoundly. "Here I am then in the Eternal City," he wrote to his brother William. "At last—for the first time—I live!" He attempted to support himself as a freelance writer in Rome, then secured a position as Paris correspondent for the New York Tribune, through the influence of its editor John Hay. When these efforts failed he returned to New York City. During 1874 and 1875 he published Transatlantic Sketches, A Passionate Pilgrim, and Roderick Hudson. During this early period in his career he was influenced by Nathaniel Hawthorne.

In 1869 he settled in London. There he established relationships with Macmillan and other publishers, who paid for serial installments that they would later publish in book form. The audience for these serialized novels was largely made up of middle-class women, and James struggled to fashion serious literary work within the strictures imposed by editors' and publishers' notions of what was suitable for young women to read. He lived in rented rooms but was able to join gentlemen's clubs that had libraries and where he could entertain male friends. He was introduced to English society by Henry Adams and Charles Milnes Gaskell, the latter introducing him to the Travellers' and the Reform Clubs.

In the fall of 1875 he moved to the Latin Quarter of Paris. Aside from two trips to America, he spent the next three decades—the rest of his life—in Europe. In Paris he met Zola, Alphonse Daudet, Maupassant, Turgenev, and others. He stayed in Paris only a year before moving to London.

In England he met the leading figures of politics and culture. He continued to be a prolific writer, producing The American (1877), The Europeans (1878), a revision of Watch and Ward (1878), French Poets and Novelists (1878), Hawthorne (1879), and several shorter works of fiction. In 1878 Daisy Miller established his fame on both sides of the Atlantic. It drew notice perhaps mostly because it depicted a woman whose behavior is outside the social norms of Europe. He also began his first masterpiece, The Portrait of a Lady, which would appear in 1881.

In 1877 he first visited Wenlock Abbey in Shropshire, home of his friend Charles Milnes Gaskell whom he had met through Henry Adams. He was much inspired by the darkly romantic Abbey and the surrounding countryside, which features in his essay Abbeys and Castles. In particular the gloomy monastic fishponds behind the Abbey are said to have inspired the lake in The Turn of the Screw.

While living in London, James continued to follow the careers of the "French realists", Émile Zola in particular. Their stylistic methods influenced his own work in the years to come. Hawthorne's influence on him faded during this period, replaced by George Eliot and Ivan Turgenev. 1879–1882 saw the publication of The Europeans, Washington Square, Confidence, and The Portrait of a Lady. He visited America in 1882–1883, then returned to London.

The period from 1881 to 1883 was marked by several losses. His mother died in 1881, followed by his father a few months later, and then by his brother Wilkie. Emerson, an old family friend, died in 1882. His friend Turgenev died in 1883.

Middle years, 1884–1897

In 1884 James made another visit to Paris. There he met again with Zola, Daudet, and Goncourt. He had been following the careers of the French "realist" or "naturalist" writers, and was increasingly influenced by them. In 1886, he published The Bostonians and The Princess Casamassima, both influenced by the French writers he'd studied assiduously. Critical reaction and sales were poor. He wrote to Howells that the books had hurt his career rather than helped because they had "reduced the desire, and demand, for my productions to zero". During this time he became friends with Robert Louis Stevenson, John Singer Sargent, Edmund Gosse, George du Maurier, Paul Bourget, and Constance Fenimore Woolson. His third novel from the 1880s was The Tragic Muse. Although he was following the precepts of Zola in his novels of the '80s, their tone and attitude are closer to the fiction of Alphonse Daudet. The lack of critical and financial success for his novels during this period led him to try writing for the theatre. (His dramatic works and his experiences with theatre are discussed below.)

In the last quarter of 1889, he started translating "for pure and copious lucre" Port Tarascon, the third volume of Alphonse Daudet adventures of Tartarin de Tarascon. Serialized in Harper's Monthly Magazine from June 1890, this translation praised as "clever" by The Spectator was published in January 1891 by Sampson Low, Marston, Searle & Rivington.

After the stage failure of Guy Domville in 1895, James was near despair and thoughts of death plagued him. The years spent on dramatic works were not entirely a loss. As he moved into the last phase of his career he found ways to adapt dramatic techniques into the novel form.

In the late 1880s and throughout the 1890s James made several trips through Europe. He spent a long stay in Italy in 1887. In that year the short novel The Aspern Papers and The Reverberator were published.

Late years, 1898–1916

In 1897–1898 he moved to Rye, Sussex, and wrote The Turn of the Screw. 1899–1900 saw the publication of The Awkward Age and The Sacred

Fount. During 1902–1904 he wrote The Ambassadors, The Wings of the Dove, and The Golden Bowl.

In 1904 he revisited America and lectured on Balzac. In 1906–1910 he published The American Scene and edited the "New York Edition", a 24-volume collection of his works. In 1910 his brother William died; Henry had just joined William from an unsuccessful search for relief in Europe on what then turned out to be his (Henry's) last visit to the United States (from summer 1910 to July 1911), and was near him, according to a letter he wrote, when he died.

In 1913 he wrote his autobiographies, A Small Boy and Others, and Notes of a Son and Brother. After the outbreak of the First World War in 1914 he did war work. In 1915 he became a British subject and was awarded the Order of Merit the following year. He died on 28 February 1916, in Chelsea, London. As he requested, his ashes were buried in Cambridge Cemetery in Massachusetts.

Biographers

James regularly rejected suggestions that he should marry, and after settling in London proclaimed himself "a bachelor". F. W. Dupee, in several volumes on the James family, originated the theory that he had been in love with his cousin Mary ("Minnie") Temple, but that a neurotic fear of sex kept him from admitting such affections: "James's invalidism ... was itself the symptom of some fear of or scruple against sexual love on his part." Dupee used an episode from James's memoir A Small Boy and Others, recounting a dream of a Napoleonic image in the Louvre, to exemplify James's romanticism about Europe, a Napoleonic fantasy into which he fled.

Dupee had not had access to the James family papers and worked principally from James's published memoir of his older brother, William, and the limited collection of letters edited by Percy Lubbock, heavily weighted toward James's last years. His account therefore moved directly from James's childhood, when he trailed after his older brother, to elderly invalidism. As more material became available to scholars, including the diaries of contemporaries and hundreds of affectionate and sometimes erotic letters

ritten by James to younger men, the picture of neurotic celibacy gave way
a portrait of a closeted homosexual.

Between 1953 and 1972, Leon Edel authored a major five-volume
iography of James, which accessed unpublished letters and documents after
del gained the permission of James's family. Edel's portrayal of James included
he suggestion he was celibate. It was a view first propounded by critic Saul
osenzweig in 1943. In 1996 Sheldon M. Novick published Henry James:
he Young Master, followed by Henry James: The Mature Master (2007).
he first book "caused something of an uproar in Jamesian circles" as it
hallenged the previous received notion of celibacy, a once-familiar paradigm
n biographies of homosexuals when direct evidence was non-existent. Novick
lso criticised Edel for following the discounted Freudian interpretation of
omosexuality "as a kind of failure." The difference of opinion erupted in
series of exchanges between Edel and Novick which were published by the
nline magazine Slate, with the latter arguing that even the suggestion of
elibacy went against James's own injunction "live!"—not "fantasize!"

A letter James wrote in old age to Hugh Walpole has been cited as an
xplicit statement of this. Walpole confessed to him of indulging in "high
nks", and James wrote a reply endorsing it: "We must know, as much as
ossible, in our beautiful art, yours & mine, what we are talking about — &
he only way to know it is to have lived & loved & cursed & floundered &
njoyed & suffered — I don't think I regret a single 'excess' of my responsive
outh".

The interpretation of James as living a less austere emotional life has
een subsequently explored by other scholars. The often intense politics
f Jamesian scholarship has also been the subject of studies. Author Colm
óibín has said that Eve Kosofsky Sedgwick's Epistemology of the Closet
ade a landmark difference to Jamesian scholarship by arguing that he be
ad as a homosexual writer whose desire to keep his sexuality a secret shaped
is layered style and dramatic artistry. According to Tóibín such a reading
removed James from the realm of dead white males who wrote about posh
eople. He became our contemporary."

James's letters to expatriate American sculptor Hendrik Christian Andersen have attracted particular attention. James met the 27-year-old Andersen in Rome in 1899, when James was 56, and wrote letters to Andersen that are intensely emotional: "I hold you, dearest boy, in my innermost love & count on your feeling me—in every throb of your soul". In a letter of 6 May 1904, to his brother William, James referred to himself as "alway your hopelessly celibate even though sexagenarian Henry". How accurate that description might have been is the subject of contention among James' biographers,   but the letters to Andersen were occasionally quasi-erotic: " put, my dear boy, my arm around you, & feel the pulsation, thereby, as it were of our excellent future & your admirable endowment." To his homosexual friend Howard Sturgis, James could write: "I repeat, almost to indiscretion, that I could live with you. Meanwhile I can only try to live without you."

His numerous letters to the many young gay men among his close male friends are more forthcoming. In a letter to Howard Sturgis, following a long visit, James refers jocularly to their "happy little congress of two" and in letters to Hugh Walpole he pursues convoluted jokes and puns about their relationship, referring to himself as an elephant who "paws you ol so benevolently" and winds about Walpole his "well meaning old trunk" His letters to Walter Berry printed by the Black Sun Press have long been celebrated for their lightly veiled eroticism.

He corresponded in almost equally extravagant language with his many female friends, writing, for example, to fellow novelist Lucy Clifford: "Dearest Lucy! What shall I say? when I love you so very, very much, and see you nine times for once that I see Others! Therefore I think that—if you want it made clear to the meanest intelligence—I love you more than I love Others." To his New York friend Mary Cadwalader Jones: "Dearest Mary Cadwalader I yearn over you, but I yearn in vain; & your long silence really breaks my heart, mystifies, depresses, almost alarms me, to the point even of making me wonder if poor unconscious & doting old Célimare [Jones's pet name for James] has 'done' anything, in some dark somnambulism of the spirit, which has ... given you a bad moment, or a wrong impression, or a 'colourable pretext' ... However these things may be, he loves you as tenderly as ever nothing, to the end of time, will ever detach him from you, & he remembers those Eleventh St. matutinal intimes hours, those telephonic matinées, as the most romantic of his life ..." His long friendship with American novelist Constance Fenimore Woolson, in whose house he lived for a number of weeks in Italy in 1887, and his shock and grief over her suicide in 1894, are discussed in detail in Edel's biography and play a central role in a study by Lyndall Gordon. (Edel conjectured that Woolson was in love with James and killed herself in part because of his coldness, but Woolson's biographers have objected to Edel's account.)

Works

Style and themes

James is one of the major figures of trans-Atlantic literature. His works frequently juxtapose characters from the Old World (Europe), embodying a feudal civilisation that is beautiful, often corrupt, and alluring, and from the New World (United States), where people are often brash, open, and assertive and embody the virtues—freedom and a more highly evolved moral character—of the new American society. James explores this clash of personalities and cultures, in stories of personal relationships in which power is exercised well or badly. His protagonists were often young American women facing oppression or abuse, and as his secretary Theodora Bosanquet remarked in her monograph Henry James at Work:

> When he walked out of the refuge of his study and into the world and looked around him, he saw a place of torment, where creatures of prey perpetually thrust their claws into the quivering flesh of doomed, defenseless children of light ... His novels are a repeated exposure of this wickedness, a reiterated and passionate plea for the fullest freedom of development, unimperiled by reckless and barbarous stupidity.

Critics have jokingly described three phases in the development of James's prose: "James I, James II, and The Old Pretender." He wrote short stories and plays. Finally, in his third and last period he returned to the long, serialised novel. Beginning in the second period, but most noticeably in the third, he increasingly abandoned direct statement in favour of frequent

149

double negatives, and complex descriptive imagery. Single paragraphs began to run for page after page, in which an initial noun would be succeeded by pronouns surrounded by clouds of adjectives and prepositional clauses, far from their original referents, and verbs would be deferred and then preceded by a series of adverbs. The overall effect could be a vivid evocation of a scene as perceived by a sensitive observer. It has been debated whether this change of style was engendered by James's shifting from writing to dictating to a typist, a change made during the composition of What Maisie Knew.

In its intense focus on the consciousness of his major characters, James's later work foreshadows extensive developments in 20th century fiction. Indeed, he might have influenced stream-of-consciousness writers such as Virginia Woolf, who not only read some of his novels but also wrote essays about them. Both contemporary and modern readers have found the late style difficult and unnecessary; his friend Edith Wharton, who admired him greatly, said that there were passages in his work that were all but incomprehensible. James was harshly portrayed by H. G. Wells as a hippopotamus laboriously attempting to pick up a pea that had got into a corner of its cage. The "late James" style was ably parodied by Max Beerbohm in "The Mote in the Middle Distance".

More important for his work overall may have been his position as an expatriate, and in other ways an outsider, living in Europe. While he came from middle-class and provincial beginnings (seen from the perspective of European polite society) he worked very hard to gain access to all levels of society, and the settings of his fiction range from working class to aristocratic, and often describe the efforts of middle-class Americans to make their way in European capitals. He confessed he got some of his best story ideas from gossip at the dinner table or at country house weekends. He worked for a living, however, and lacked the experiences of select schools, university, and army service, the common bonds of masculine society. He was furthermore a man whose tastes and interests were, according to the prevailing standards of Victorian era Anglo-American culture, rather feminine, and who was shadowed by the cloud of prejudice that then and later accompanied suspicions of his homosexuality. Edmund Wilson famously compared James's objectivity to Shakespeare's:

One would be in a position to appreciate James better if one compared him with the dramatists of the seventeenth century—Racine and Molière, whom he resembles in form as well as in point of view, and even Shakespeare, when allowances are made for the most extreme differences in subject and form. These poets are not, like Dickens and Hardy, writers of melodrama—either humorous or pessimistic, nor secretaries of society like Balzac, nor prophets like Tolstoy: they are occupied simply with the presentation of conflicts of moral character, which they do not concern themselves about softening or averting. They do not indict society for these situations: they regard them as universal and inevitable. They do not even blame God for allowing them: they accept them as the conditions of life.

It is also possible to see many of James's stories as psychological thought-experiments. In his preface to the New York edition of The American he describes the development of the story in his mind as exactly such: the "situation" of an American, "some robust but insidiously beguiled and betrayed, some cruelly wronged, compatriot..." with the focus of the story being on the response of this wronged man. The Portrait of a Lady may be an experiment to see what happens when an idealistic young woman suddenly becomes very rich. In many of his tales, characters seem to exemplify alternative futures and possibilities, as most markedly in "The Jolly Corner", in which the protagonist and a ghost-doppelganger live alternative American and European lives; and in others, like The Ambassadors, an older James seems fondly to regard his own younger self facing a crucial moment.

Major novels

The first period of James's fiction, usually considered to have culminated in The Portrait of a Lady, concentrated on the contrast between Europe and America. The style of these novels is generally straightforward and, though personally characteristic, well within the norms of 19th-century fiction. Roderick Hudson (1875) is a Künstlerroman that traces the development of the title character, an extremely talented sculptor. Although the book shows some signs of immaturity—this was James's first serious attempt at a full-length novel—it has attracted favourable comment due to the vivid realisation of the three major characters: Roderick Hudson, superbly gifted but unstable and unreliable; Rowland Mallet, Roderick's limited but much more mature friend and patron; and Christina Light, one of James's most enchanting and maddening femmes fatales. The pair of Hudson and Mallet has been seen as representing the two sides of James's own nature: the wildly imaginative artist and the brooding conscientious mentor.

In The Portrait of a Lady (1881) James concluded the first phase of his career with a novel that remains his most popular piece of long fiction. The story is of a spirited young American woman, Isabel Archer, who "affronts her destiny" and finds it overwhelming. She inherits a large amount of money and subsequently becomes the victim of Machiavellian scheming by two American expatriates. The narrative is set mainly in Europe, especially in England and Italy. Generally regarded as the masterpiece of his early phase, The Portrait of a Lady is described as a psychological novel, exploring the minds of his characters, and almost a work of social science, exploring the differences between Europeans and Americans, the old and the new worlds.

The second period of James's career, which extends from the publication of The Portrait of a Lady through the end of the nineteenth century, features less popular novels including The Princess Casamassima, published serially in The Atlantic Monthly in 1885–1886, and The Bostonians, published serially in The Century Magazine during the same period. This period also featured James's celebrated Gothic novella, The Turn of the Screw.

The third period of James's career reached its most significant achievement in three novels published just around the start of the 20th century: The Wings of the Dove (1902), The Ambassadors (1903), and The Golden Bowl (1904). Critic F. O. Matthiessen called this "trilogy" James's major phase, and these novels have certainly received intense critical study. It was the second-written of the books, The Wings of the Dove (1902) that was the first published because it attracted no serialization. This novel tells the story of Milly Theale, an American heiress stricken with a serious disease, and her impact on the people around her. Some of these people befriend Milly with honourable motives, while others are more self-interested. James

ated in his autobiographical books that Milly was based on Minny Temple,
is beloved cousin who died at an early age of tuberculosis. He said that he
tempted in the novel to wrap her memory in the "beauty and dignity of
t".

Shorter narratives

James was particularly interested in what he called the "beautiful and
lest nouvelle", or the longer form of short narrative. Still, he produced a
umber of very short stories in which he achieved notable compression of
ometimes complex subjects. The following narratives are representative of
mes's achievement in the shorter forms of fiction.

- "A Tragedy of Error" (1864), short story

- "The Story of a Year" (1865), short story

- A Passionate Pilgrim (1871), novella

- Madame de Mauves (1874), novella

- Daisy Miller (1878), novella

- The Aspern Papers (1888), novella

- The Lesson of the Master (1888), novella

- The Pupil (1891), short story

- "The Figure in the Carpet" (1896), short story

- The Beast in the Jungle (1903), novella

- An International Episode (1878)

- Picture and Text

- Four Meetings (1885)

- A London Life, and Other Tales (1889)

- The Spoils of Poynton (1896)

- Embarrassments (1896)

- The Two Magics: The Turn of the Screw, Covering End (1898)

- A Little Tour of France (1900)

- The Sacred Fount (1901)

- Views and Reviews (1908)

- The Wings of the Dove, Volume I (1902)

- The Wings of the Dove, Volume II (1909)

- The Finer Grain (1910)

- The Outcry (1911)

- Lady Barbarina: The Siege of London, An International Episode and Other Tales (1922)

- The Birthplace (1922)

Plays

At several points in his career James wrote plays, beginning with one-act plays written for periodicals in 1869 and 1871 and a dramatisation of his popular novella Daisy Miller in 1882. From 1890 to 1892, having received a bequest that freed him from magazine publication, he made a strenuous effort to succeed on the London stage, writing a half-dozen plays of which only one, a dramatisation of his novel The American, was produced. This play was performed for several years by a touring repertory company and had a respectable run in London, but did not earn very much money for James. His other plays written at this time were not produced.

In 1893, however, he responded to a request from actor-manager George Alexander for a serious play for the opening of his renovated St James's Theatre, and wrote a long drama, Guy Domville, which Alexander produced. There was a noisy uproar on the opening night, 5 January 1895 with hissing from the gallery when James took his bow after the final curtain and the author was upset. The play received moderately good reviews and had a modest run of four weeks before being taken off to make way for Oscar Wilde's The Importance of Being Earnest, which Alexander thought would have better prospects for the coming season.

After the stresses and disappointment of these efforts James insisted that he would write no more for the theatre, but within weeks had agreed to write a curtain-raiser for Ellen Terry. This became the one-act "Summersoft", which he later rewrote into a short story, "Covering End", and then expanded into a full-length play, The High Bid, which had a brief run in London in 1907, when James made another concerted effort to write for the stage. He wrote three new plays, two of which were in production when the death of Edward VII on 6 May 1910 plunged London into mourning and theatres closed. Discouraged by failing health and the stresses of theatrical work, James did not renew his efforts in the theatre, but recycled his plays as successful novels. The Outcry was a best-seller in the United States when it was published in 1911. During the years 1890–1893 when he was most engaged with the theatre, James wrote a good deal of theatrical criticism and assisted Elizabeth Robins and others in translating and producing Henrik Ibsen for the first time in London.

Leon Edel argued in his psychoanalytic biography that James was traumatised by the opening night uproar that greeted Guy Domville, and that it plunged him into a prolonged depression. The successful later novels, in Edel's view, were the result of a kind of self-analysis, expressed in fiction, which partly freed him from his fears. Other biographers and scholars have not accepted this account, however; the more common view being that of F.O. Matthiessen, who wrote: "Instead of being crushed by the collapse of his hopes [for the theatre]... he felt a resurgence of new energy."

Non-fiction

Beyond his fiction, James was one of the more important literary critics in the history of the novel. In his classic essay The Art of Fiction (1884), he argued against rigid prescriptions on the novelist's choice of subject and method of treatment. He maintained that the widest possible freedom in content and approach would help ensure narrative fiction's continued vitality.

155

James wrote many valuable critical articles on other novelists; typical is his book-length study of Nathaniel Hawthorne, which has been the subject of critical debate. Richard Brodhead has suggested that the study was emblematic of James's struggle with Hawthorne's influence, and constituted an effort to place the elder writer "at a disadvantage." Gordon Fraser, meanwhile, has suggested that the study was part of a more commercial effort by James to introduce himself to British readers as Hawthorne's natural successor.

When James assembled the New York Edition of his fiction in his final years, he wrote a series of prefaces that subjected his own work to searching, occasionally harsh criticism.

At 22 James wrote The Noble School of Fiction for The Nation's first issue in 1865. He would write, in all, over 200 essays and book, art, and theatre reviews for the magazine.

For most of his life James harboured ambitions for success as a playwright. He converted his novel The American into a play that enjoyed modest returns in the early 1890s. In all he wrote about a dozen plays, most of which went unproduced. His costume drama Guy Domville failed disastrously on its opening night in 1895. James then largely abandoned his efforts to conquer the stage and returned to his fiction. In his Notebooks he maintained that his theatrical experiment benefited his novels and tales by helping him dramatise his characters' thoughts and emotions. James produced a small but valuable amount of theatrical criticism, including perceptive appreciations of Henrik Ibsen.

With his wide-ranging artistic interests, James occasionally wrote on the visual arts. Perhaps his most valuable contribution was his favourable assessment of fellow expatriate John Singer Sargent, a painter whose critical status has improved markedly in recent decades. James also wrote sometimes charming, sometimes brooding articles about various places he visited and lived in. His most famous books of travel writing include Italian Hours (an example of the charming approach) and The American Scene (most definitely on the brooding side).

James was one of the great letter-writers of any era. More than ten thousand of his personal letters are extant, and over three thousand have been published in a large number of collections. A complete edition of James's letters began publication in 2006, edited by Pierre Walker and Greg Zacharias. As of 2014, eight volumes have been published, covering the period from 1855 to 1880. James's correspondents included celebrated contemporaries like Robert Louis Stevenson, Edith Wharton and Joseph Conrad, along with many others in his wide circle of friends and acquaintances. The letters range from the "mere twaddle of graciousness" to serious discussions of artistic, social and personal issues.

Very late in life James began a series of autobiographical works: A Small Boy and Others, Notes of a Son and Brother, and the unfinished The Middle Years. These books portray the development of a classic observer who was passionately interested in artistic creation but was somewhat reticent about participating fully in the life around him.

Reception

Criticism, biographies and fictional treatments

James's work has remained steadily popular with the limited audience of educated readers to whom he spoke during his lifetime, and has remained firmly in the canon, but, after his death, some American critics, such as Van Wyck Brooks, expressed hostility towards James for his long expatriation and eventual naturalisation as a British subject. Other critics such as E. M. Forster complained about what they saw as James's squeamishness in the treatment of sex and other possibly controversial material, or dismissed his late style as difficult and obscure, relying heavily on extremely long sentences and excessively latinate language. Similarly Oscar Wilde criticised him for writing "fiction as if it were a painful duty". Vernon Parrington, composing a canon of American literature, condemned James for having cut himself off from America. Jorge Luis Borges wrote about him, "Despite the scruples and delicate complexities of James, his work suffers from a major defect: the absence of life." And Virginia Woolf, writing to Lytton Strachey, asked, "Please tell me what you find in Henry James. ... we have his works here, and

I read, and I can't find anything but faintly tinged rose water, urbane and sleek, but vulgar and pale as Walter Lamb. Is there really any sense in it?" The novelist W. Somerset Maugham wrote, "He did not know the English as an Englishman instinctively knows them and so his English characters never to my mind quite ring true," and argued "The great novelists, even in seclusion, have lived life passionately. Henry James was content to observe it from a window." Maugham nevertheless wrote, "The fact remains that those last novels of his, notwithstanding their unreality, make all other novels, except the very best, unreadable." Colm Tóibín observed that James "never really wrote about the English very well. His English characters don't work for me."

Despite these criticisms, James is now valued for his psychological and moral realism, his masterful creation of character, his low-key but playful humour, and his assured command of the language. In his 1983 book, The Novels of Henry James, Edward Wagenknecht offers an assessment that echoes Theodora Bosanquet's:

> "To be completely great," Henry James wrote in an early review, "a work of art must lift up the heart," and his own novels do this to an outstanding degree ... More than sixty years after his death, the great novelist who sometimes professed to have no opinions stands foursquare in the great Christian humanistic and democratic tradition. The men and women who, at the height of World War II, raided the secondhand shops for his out-of-print books knew what they were about. For no writer ever raised a braver banner to which all who love freedom might adhere.

William Dean Howells saw James as a representative of a new realist school of literary art which broke with the English romantic tradition epitomised by the works of Charles Dickens and William Makepeace Thackeray. Howells wrote that realism found "its chief exemplar in Mr. James... A novelist he is not, after the old fashion, or after any fashion but his own." F.R. Leavis championed Henry James as a novelist of "established pre-eminence" in The Great Tradition (1948), asserting that The Portrait of a Lady and The Bostonians were "the two most brilliant novels in the language." James is now prized as a master of point of view who moved literary fiction forward by insisting in showing, not telling, his stories to the reader. (Source: Wikipedia)

NOTABLE WORKS

NOVELS

Watch and Ward (1871)

Roderick Hudson (1875)

The American (1877)

The Europeans (1878)

Confidence (1879)

Washington Square (1880)

The Portrait of a Lady (1881)

The Bostonians (1886)

The Princess Casamassima (1886)

The Reverberator (1888)

The Tragic Muse (1890)

The Other House (1896)

The Spoils of Poynton (1897)

What Maisie Knew (1897)

The Awkward Age (1899)

The Sacred Fount (1901)

The Wings of the Dove (1902)

The Ambassadors (1903)

The Golden Bowl (1904)

The Whole Family (collaborative novel with eleven other authors, 1908

The Outcry (1911)

The Ivory Tower (unfinished, published posthumously 1917)

The Sense of the Past (unfinished, published posthumously 1917)

SHORT STORIES AND NOVELLAS

A Tragedy of Error (1864)

The Story of a Year (1865)

A Landscape Painter (1866)

A Day of Days (1866)

My Friend Bingham (1867)

Poor Richard (1867)

The Story of a Masterpiece (1868)

A Most Extraordinary Case (1868)

A Problem (1868)

De Grey: A Romance (1868)

Osborne's Revenge (1868)

The Romance of Certain Old Clothes (1868)

A Light Man (1869)

Gabrielle de Bergerac (1869)

Travelling Companions (1870)

A Passionate Pilgrim (1871)

At Isella (1871)

Master Eustace (1871)

Guest's Confession (1872)

The Madonna of the Future (1873)

The Sweetheart of M. Briseux (1873)

The Last of the Valerii (1874)

Madame de Mauves (1874)

Adina (1874)

Professor Fargo (1874)

Eugene Pickering (1874)

Benvolio (1875)

Crawford's Consistency (1876)

The Ghostly Rental (1876)

Four Meetings (1877)

Rose-Agathe (1878, as Théodolinde)

Daisy Miller (1878)

Longstaff's Marriage (1878)

An International Episode (1878)

The Pension Beaurepas (1879)

A Diary of a Man of Fifty (1879)

A Bundle of Letters (1879)

The Point of View (1882)

The Siege of London (1883)

Impressions of a Cousin (1883)

Lady Barberina (1884)

Pandora (1884)

The Author of Beltraffio (1884)

Georgina's Reasons (1884)

A New England Winter (1884)

The Path of Duty (1884)

Mrs. Temperly (1887)

Louisa Pallant (1888)

The Aspern Papers (1888)

The Liar (1888)

The Modern Warning (1888, originally published as The Two Countries)

A London Life (1888)

The Patagonia (1888)

The Lesson of the Master (1888)

The Solution (1888)

The Pupil (1891)

Brooksmith (1891)

The Marriages (1891)

The Chaperon (1891)

Sir Edmund Orme (1891)

Nona Vincent (1892)

The Real Thing (1892)

The Private Life (1892)

Lord Beaupré (1892)

The Visits (1892)

Sir Dominick Ferrand (1892)

Greville Fane (1892)

Collaboration (1892)

Owen Wingrave (1892)

The Wheel of Time (1892)

The Middle Years (1893)

The Death of the Lion (1894)

The Coxon Fund (1894)

The Next Time (1895)

Glasses (1896)

The Altar of the Dead (1895)

The Figure in the Carpet (1896)

The Way It Came (1896, also published as The Friends of the Friends)

The Turn of the Screw (1898)

Covering End (1898)

In the Cage (1898)

John Delavoy (1898)

The Given Case (1898)

Europe (1899)

The Great Condition (1899)

The Real Right Thing (1899)

Paste (1899)

The Great Good Place (1900)

Maud-Evelyn (1900)

Miss Gunton of Poughkeepsie (1900)

The Tree of Knowledge (1900)

The Abasement of the Northmores (1900)

The Third Person (1900)

The Special Type (1900)

The Tone of Time (1900)

Broken Wings (1900)

The Two Faces (1900)

Mrs. Medwin (1901)

The Beldonald Holbein (1901)

The Story in It (1902)

Flickerbridge (1902)

The Birthplace (1903)

The Beast in the Jungle (1903)

The Papers (1903)

Fordham Castle (1904)

Julia Bride (1908)

The Jolly Corner (1908)

The Velvet Glove (1909)

Mora Montravers (1909)

Crapy Cornelia (1909)

The Bench of Desolation (1909)

A Round of Visits (1910)

<u>OTHER</u>

Transatlantic Sketches (1875)

French Poets and Novelists (1878)

Hawthorne (1879)

Portraits of Places (1883)

A Little Tour in France (1884)

Partial Portraits (1888)

Essays in London and Elsewhere (1893)

Picture and Text (1893)

Terminations (1893)

Theatricals (1894)

Theatricals: Second Series (1895)

Guy Domville (1895)

The Soft Side (1900)

William Wetmore Story and His Friends (1903)

The Better Sort (1903)

English Hours (1905)

The Question of our Speech; The Lesson of Balzac. Two Lectures (1905)

The American Scene (1907)

Views and Reviews (1908)

Italian Hours (1909)

A Small Boy and Others (1913)

Notes on Novelists (1914)

Notes of a Son and Brother (1914)

Within the Rim (1918)

Travelling Companions (1919)

Notebooks (various, published posthumously)

The Middle Years (unfinished, published posthumously 1917)

A Most Unholy Trade (1925, published posthumously)

The Art of the Novel : Critical Prefaces (1934)

CPSIA information can be obtained
at www.ICGtesting.com
Printed in the USA
LVHW052044021120
670493LV00002B/29